THE FLIPSIDE FILES 1

VALERIE BROOK

SPIRIT HOUSE Books

The Flipside Files 1

Published by Spirit House Books

The Ball Breaker's Summer Club first published in *Fiction River: Justice*, edited by Kristine Kathryn Rusch, 2018; *The Disinvention of the Surveillance State* first published in *Fiction River: Editor's Choice*, edited by Kristine Kathryn Rusch, 2018; *The Chicken Time Machine* first published in *Pulphouse Fiction Magazine*, edited by Dean Wesley Smith, 2018; *Mother Rock Mamba* first published as *The One Left* in *Pulphouse Fiction Magazine*, edited by Dean Wesley Smith, 2018; *The Dust Devil, the Riffraff, and the Big Orange Sunset* first published in *Fiction River: Visions of the Apocalypse*, edited by John Helfers, 2016; *The Sea Girl's Survival* first published by *Pulphouse Fiction Magazine*, 2018; *The Ordinary* first published in *Fiction River: Superpowers*, edited by Rebecca Moesta, 2017

Second Edition
Hardback ISBN#: 978-1-942026-14-3
Papaerback ISBN#: 978-1-942026-13-6
10 9 8 7 6 5 4 3 2

CONTENTS

INTRODUCTION

I am excited to present *The Flipside Files* as a diverse and ongoing collection of my short fiction.

Many of these stories have a defining choice at its core —choices that transform destinies. You can expect unique and resilient characters who tackle adversity and prevail despite the odds. Perhaps one day some of the characters in these short tales will go on having further adventures in novels of their own.

But for now, sit down and buckle up; you're in for a wild ride.

—Valerie Brook
Las Vegas, NV

THE BALL BREAKER'S SUMMER CLUB

THE FIRST MORNING of summer vacation seriously needs big fluffy buttermilk pancakes, so you can celebrate, like right out of the Oprah magazines on the bottom rack of the Quick 'N Go.

Without the buttermilk, actually.

Because I can't stand that sour stuff. But you know what I mean.

All my stepmom, I mean my step-not-mom, had in the pantry was box yellow cake mix, so I was currently fighting with the only spatula we owned and proving to a point that non-stick is a lie.

Ruby rang my cell phone and it vibrated off the counter and fell into the bowl of wet brown dog food on the floor in the rainbow plastic bowl.

Now, that tells you something when Wiener, my big giant fat wiener dog, sniffed the food last night and walked away from it.

I pulled the Nokia out of the dog blob and wiped my

pay-as-you-go phone off with a paper towel. I'm just trying to say that it's cheap, not that we're poor and it's all we can afford.

"Don't do that," I said. "Now I have to talk to you and my phone smells like human mouth."

"What?" Ruby whispered. "Don't even start with that bacteria thing again, Felicia. I know the molecular world is a new discovery for you and all, but sixth grade science is over. I need you here, pronto."

"As in right now?" I said, looking woefully at my celebratory breakfast. Even though it smelled wonderful it actually looked a bit like vomit in the pan, and for that reason only I'm sure Oprah would not eat it. I slid the hot pan onto a cold burner.

"No, yesterday."

I paused to think about that. "That's impossible."

"Just get over here."

It's really easy to go to Ruby's house. I walked out the front door of our single wide trailer in the park, sponged across the fake outdoor golf-course-grass carpet mat which is mysteriously always soggy, hopped over the two-foot white plastic garden fence for which we have no garden, and looked up at her faded pink trailer door.

I'm not allowed to knock anymore.

Ruby lives alone with her grumpy dad and he got a new job at the graveyard doing shifts. He has about the personality of Mr. Potato Head the toy. The last time I knocked he answered the door in his Christmas boxers and yelled at me in Cuban Spanish, which has English in it, and I never knew men could grow so much hair there.

I mean on his back.

It makes you wonder about the theory of evolution and maybe the missing link is not actually missing anymore.

Anyway, I promised myself not to see Mr. Vazquez mostly naked again. One time did it enough for me.

I saw movement to my right and Ruby's face enlarged like a magnifying glass in the window to the right of the door. Ruby has really beautiful brown skin and I'm just white as a ghost.

It kinda sucks that way, but we can't like everything about ourselves. I do have really pretty shoulders. I've been told that before.

Ruby gave me the five minute hand signal, then disappeared. I'm like, really? Because I could have finished cooking and eating by then.

So I ran back over to my house and finished cooking and eating and came back over to her house.

She opened the door and flew out like a bird because she's as skinny as a piece of graph paper. She could practically be an origami doll all folded up and intricate, but super functional just the same.

"What on earth are you so excited about?" I said. It was Saturday morning around ten o'clock and the whole octagonal trailer park was shrouded in an awkward summer mist. This is what we get for living in Arcata on the damp northern California coast.

We're like the survivors of a lost continent out here. And when the wind blows right, the air also smells like cow patties from the pasture and the pulp mill.

I won't tell you what the pulp mill smells like.

Well, it's basically poop, too.

"Look," she said. From the pocket of her purple velvet lounge jacket she pulled out a tiny little blue plastic chip with copper squares. I knew immediately it was a memory card. And belonging to the Cannon PowerShot SD780 IS.

It has 12.1 megapixels. And shoots video.

"OMG," I said, just like if we were texting. "You found it?"

Ruby nodded in that *I know something you don't* kind of way, her eyes all narrowed and spicy and conspiratorial. Just like a janitor would look who had just found a diamond ring in the lunchroom trash can and slinked it into a secret compartment on the end of his mop.

"It had some old toothpaste on it, but I wiped it off," she said. I took that to mean it got lost in the bathroom.

She raised her eyebrows twice and that's the signal for getting on our garage sale bikes and going somewhere fun. In this case, we both knew exactly where we were going without saying.

So we raced off running toward our bikes, which are sandwiched together with a heavy chain-link that loops around the leg of the wooden picnic bench, which was like five steps from where we were already standing.

I won.

We never actually lock up our bikes anymore because the Master Lock got so rusty we threw it away, but we do drape the chain around the tires and it looks exactly the same.

"Last one there is a rotten egg," I said.

We hopped the curb onto Manmaker Lane and put the

pedal to the metal. The downtown streets were so quiet and lazy we were able to do figure-eights through the middle of the white line down the street.

Did you ever see that movie where there were fog people in it? You really can't see anything until it's practically too late and you're smack in front of it.

Then I suddenly realized there was a huge flaw in our whole plan. Like how could we be so stupid.

"Stop," I yelled breathlessly. Ruby squeezed her brakes right in front of me and I practically creamed her. I skidded to the left just in time. That's a sore spot of an argument between us, "the stopping too fast in front of the other person" thing.

So I just let it go this time in the spirit of chivalry.

"How the hell are we going to record anything in this weather?" I said. "What are you thinking?"

Ruby nodded in that way again, the spicy *I know something you don't* way.

She always looks like a movie star when she does that. A cool Cuban cucumber.

If we were in a movie together, I'd rather do the lighting or do the sound. I could give her hand signals from backstage to help her out if she was messing up—like forgetting her lines.

We already decided we have to have the same career when we grow up, but it's okay to work in a different *aspect* of that career. That way, we will always have our own individual lives, which I think is important.

Getting back to the point, Ruby explained that we

weren't going to our Infamous Technotronic Treehouse like I thought we *both* thought we were.

No, we're going to ground zero—Mr. Winker's actual house.

Because Ruby explained, last night when her dad was driving her home from after-school super detention, which is thirty minutes longer than regular detention, she actually *saw* Mrs. Peabody's car parked behind Mr. Winker's house.

"It's the moment we've been waiting eons for," Ruby said. "Proof that they are cheating with each other. Come on let's do a stakeout."

My eyes widened. We'd been on Mr. Winker's tail ever since he separated our seats in biology class for texting each other. We weren't texting. We did happen to be accidentally surfing the internet at the exact same moment, but it was just a coincidence.

He didn't care.

Well, he should have cared because one of our top career options is Private Detective, and we'll have our offices in a duplex and work out of the opposite sides on cases. But before you go to college to become learned on a subject, you first should try it out and make sure it's up your alley.

Pedal to the metal again and we raced up Old Buttermilk Lane though the swirling sheets of mist. There were some hints of blue sky but then it would vanish. Riding your bike fast though cool mist is refreshing for your face.

It's almost like a facelift I would imagine.

We hid our bikes in the blackberry bushes and tried to

act natural walking a few blocks up a hill in the nicer neighborhood. I whistled and Ruby gazed upwards at the redwoods that are like one-legged tree giants that are standing on one leg.

I guess that's redundant.

Wow, some of these kids get things like trampolines and jungle gyms in their backyards.

And those BBQ grills that open like a silver treasure chest, I'm just saying that's one big piece of steak that can fit in there. Middle-class people can get like better cuts of meat and stuff.

When Mr. Winkler's ocean blue house with a brick chimney puffing wood smoke like a whale spout came into view, Ruby yanked my elbow and pulled me down behind a huge parked RV with a black spandex tarp over the top of it.

I was now crouched shoulder to shoulder with Ruby. Her purple velvet lounge jacket is very awesome but the fuzzy stuff on her hood reached out and irritated my neck. I looked in her eyes like *why did you pull me?* She nodded her head twice. That's the signal for when we are in danger of getting caught for something, and you can nod your head anywhere from one time up to nine.

And if it's at nine, then we're pretty much for sure going to federal prison.

But just two nods—that's merely on par with super detention.

We were actually on somebody's property now, squatting on the outskirts of their driveway by the concrete sidewalk. Behind our butts there were four nice and tidy trashcans and a properly astute natural wood fence.

I couldn't even see Mr. Winkler's brick chimney house anymore, just spandex at the tip of my nose.

I wasn't sure what the danger was but I didn't want to ask in case my voice gave our location away, so I just waited silently on my haunches. Sometimes Ruby really takes the lead with things and you just gotta let her do it. She was peering around the corner of the RV, pointing the Canon SuperShot down the street like a real detective would.

I could hear the little shutter going *whizbang*. Or whatever a digital shutter sounds like in spelling.

Then I noticed there was a dimple in the spandex where it kinda pulled up like somebody had been accidentally pointing their blow dryer on the spandex and it had gotten too hot, melted a little, and curled up on itself.

I tapped Ruby's shoulder and she didn't respond. *Whizbang. Whizbang.*

So I got flat on my belly and crawled in like a bear going into a cave. Or I guess more like a lizard going into a narrow opening that you can only be a lizard to fit into.

It's kinda creepy to be underneath a machine like that all shrouded in a black material that's sweeping the concrete like a bed skirt. The hairs on the back of my neck went up because I was thinking what if in a freak accident all four tires go flat at the same time right now and I start getting crushed like that famous trash compactor scene in *Star Wars.* That's a really great movie by the way, if you haven't seen it.

I think they even made a sequel.

A few seconds later Ruby was under the RV with me. "Great idea," she whispered.

You know, what does RV even stand for? Remote Vehicle? That doesn't make sense. Rectangular Vehicle?

"Did you get the license plate?" I whispered.

Ruby nodded enthusiastically, so much so that she cracked her head on a metallic thingamabob coming out of the engine. But at that exact moment there was another noise.

A shout.

Like an angry man just mangled a word. Glass shattered like an explosion. A door slammed.

Ruby and I started army soldier crawling on our elbows toward the voice so we could see what was going on, which was up toward the engine area and closer to the residence.

We didn't know who lived here, but they sure did have a home security issue with the spandex. It was like military-grade camo. One hundred CIA agents could fit under here practically and no one would ever know they were here.

Ruby had her camera in hand and I knew what she was thinking.

I reached out and delicately lifted the spandex skirt like a mouse. We were in the perfect angle to see under the chain-link fence that the RV was nosed up against. The concrete driveway continued forward until it dead-ended at a shed that had a closed door and one small window with a wrinkled white curtain that looked like a bandaged black eye.

"You goddam piece of shit," a beefy man said. He had a belly like a bulldozer. He was actually wearing a wife-beater tank top with the armpits a little bit yellow and some new dark blue Levis jeans. He had better control of himself after that shout. His voice was quiet and cruel now. "The fuck I tell you about it?"

Then my eyes caught movement to the far right.

There was a kid on his butt like he'd been shoved down. He was wearing pajama bottoms with armored badass Ninja Turtles but his chest and feet were naked and undefended.

His face twisted, his pale lips barred back in a grimace of desperation.

There was green beer bottle glass all around the kid's body as he crept back on his palms. Some of the swirling mist had lifted right then and a moment of blue sunny sky coughed up some rays of light that made the glass shards twinkle like diamonds.

Except for the red ooze of blood.

It pooled out from under his left hand.

The boy's eyes looked hollowed out and filled up black with dread. Also like a deer in headlights unable to run. And even like that kid Blake who I saw at recess sometimes and who was a grade younger.

It *was* Blake.

I heard *whizbang*.

Then the particular sound of the beefy man's black

leather belt whipping off. It's like *shhhh* and *hiss* put together, or a super bad snake.

I started to smell a cringeworthy smell, and I think it was coming off my neck. I felt suddenly like a stink beetle, the shiny round black kind with long legs. When you scare one it emits a nasty odor that smells like an intestinal surgery gone wrong.

Now the beefy man loomed over the kid.

The man jerked his head to the left like he was silently saying get into the shed you brat.

Blake crawled up on his bare feet, trying to miss the glass landmines. He walked the plank to the shed door, opened it, and was swallowed inside.

The beefy man with the belt followed.

The shed door slammed and locked.

I realized my lungs were aching like I'd inhaled two bowling balls and they were stuck in my chest.

"That's Blake," I managed to whisper to Ruby. But when I turned toward her she was already halfway scooted out of the spandex skirt right out into enemy territory. My nose brushed her ankles.

Geez, that kid scoots faster than a real army soldier. Then I realized it wasn't that she scoots fast, it's that I was paralyzed in place. I mean, I could have peed my pants and not even felt it.

"Ruby," I said in that hard whisper that means *get back here right now.*

But Ruby was now in extreme Private Detective mode, which is much more advanced than normal Private Detective mode. She crawled under the high chain-link fence because she's the size of a piece of paper, slunk alongside the house past the side door, and then disappeared behind the shed with a purple flash.

I could have died and turned to fossil for as heavy with dread I felt.

Relaxation Vehicle? Damn. That RV word was stumping me.

When you're paralyzed time really slows down. I think like five minutes passed and I only had one real thought.

I heard a high-pitched commotion and Ruby whipped back around the corner of the shed with a pink chihuahua in a tutu snapping at her heels.

I'm not kidding.

When Ruby dove back under the spandex skirt we both would have nodded our heads nine times to indicate federal prison-level danger, but there wasn't enough time.

We wormed our way back out to the public sidewalk, hurried back to the blackberry patch where the mist still swirled, and got out of Dodge on our bikes like they had rocket blasters belching fire and the fog people from that one movie I can't remember were lumbering toward us like zombie prison guards dangling *got-ya* handcuffs.

WE DIDN'T STOP PEDALING UNTIL WE SKIDDED TO THE CURB AT the secret trail entrance to our Infamous Technotronic Treehouse behind the all-night Safeway grocery store.

My throat burned raw and my cheeks felt so red they probably would show up on a satellite image.

The back end of the big buildings are snug up against Highway 101, but there's prime real estate between the mushy drainage ditch and the garbage bins beside the loading docks.

I think it always smells like doughnuts.

We pushed our bikes along the muddy trail through the blackberry bushes. Did you know they are an invasive species?

There's a giant old pine tree and last summer we nailed together a room off the ground with old pallets that we drug out here from the Dumpsters. A saw, two hammers, and a bunch of nails from the back of Ruby's dad's truck, plus a green tarp roof that he'll never notice is missing, and *wha-la* we have our offices.

Love it.

We even put an old green Army sleeping bag from Goodwill inside, and an egg crate for padding. The outside wall has a no trespassing sign.

After Christmas we super scored while Dumpster diving and got like a million rainbow indoor tree lights. So now on special days we check to see if the coast is clear and run out with our orange extension cord and plug into Safeway.

They haven't caught us yet.

It's only like one nod on the risk-nodding scale of danger.

The Christmas lights twinkled in a disco dance across Ruby's face as she explained that she had circled the shed but hadn't found another window to take any pictures or get evidence.

And the pink barking chihuahua had run out of a pet door from the main house.

And come hell or high water we weren't going to let Mr. Beefy get away with child abuse. Our parents sucked but they didn't abuse us.

The privileged need to look out for the underprivileged.

We agreed to tail Blake until we caught him alone and came up with a plan to help. We weren't sure how to explain how we witnessed him being abused without sounding creepy, but we did agree to add in the career option of Counselor to our list.

IT TURNED OUT TO BE HARD TO TAIL BLAKE.

As a side note, every single car on the planet can accelerate away from your bicycle like a torpedo. So don't try to follow one with the idea you'll catch up at stop signs.

It took a week to figure out Blake takes gymnastic lessons on Tuesday afternoon. Then he plays video games at the Pizzaria 'N Kabob Shop with his little five-year-old brother Albert while he waits for his mom to pick him up.

Ruby and I were incognito in dark sunglasses at a table in a corner under the widescreen TV that only played MTV music videos from the eighties. Ruby swears it's in a time warp, like a real one.

I'm not sure we should sit next to the TV, just in case it includes us, too.

I monitor Ruby every time we come in here just to make sure she doesn't suggest we go out and get perms.

We decided to split up and left our Cokes dripping moisture rings over the waitress's dirty rag streaks on the table. I grabbed my school backpack, which was enormously heavy at this point and threatening to rip at the seams, and Ruby headed toward the only other table with a patron, where Albert sat eating a wedge of greasy pizza.

I rounded the corner into the video game room where Pac Man and Donkey Kong warbled their musical bleeps through speakers that sounded like they had drown with the Lost City of Atlantis.

"Hey, Blake," I said to Blake, who was thrusting a joystick every which direction like he was trying to shake pineapples out of a tree.

He didn't even respond.

Wait, is his name not even Blake? No, for sure his name is Blake.

"Remember me from school?"

I noticed a swatch of Band-Aids on his left palm. His spaceship exploded and the glow from the screen colored his skin green.

"Remember I walked into the boys' bathroom once," I said, "and you were like, hey, this is the boys' bathroom. And we laughed and you gave me a cinnamon Altoid?"

Blake turned his brooding, arcade-games-suck eyes up at me. A spark of recognition lit up his face and he turned happy. "Oh hey, Felicia," he said. "What 'sup?"

Being that I'm testing out the career option of Private Detective plus Counselor, I did not come unprepared.

Once a month, if you shake the giant gum ball machine by the exit doors to Safeway after the janitor has unplugged it to vacuum the dust and trash that accumulates behind it during said month, you might find that it dispenses *quarters* instead of gum.

I discovered this quite on purpose.

"Do you want to share my quarters?" I said. I heaved the backpack on top the joystick on the arcade game and unzipped my booty.

Wait, I mean bounty, as in the pirate stuff.

Blake's eyes widened like we were looking at nuggets of gold and glittering jewels. "Wow," he whispered.

It *was* kinda awesome, in fact. Like maybe we could all afford to live inside the Pizzaria 'N Kabob Shop for weeks if there was an apocalypse. "Do you and your little brother wanna join mine and Ruby's club? It's like a justice club. We even have a treehouse."

He was like sure.

See? Money talks or people walk. Clint Eastwood said that.

When Blake and his brother Albert rode their bikes to meet us at the Infamous Technotronic Treehouse three days later on a blue-sky afternoon, Ruby brought a box of saltines and grape jam and the four of us munched away like rodents.

"It's like a glow-in-the-dark disco cave in here," Blake said in awe. "You just need some dance music."

Ruby explained our radio broke last month.

Blake was wearing concealing long pants and a long T-shirt and the rest of us were in leg revealing shorts. There was still a swatch of Band-Aids across his palm, though the bandages were dirty and crinkled but still adhered.

I guess that shows how sticky that Band-Aid brand can really be.

The idea of Scientific Chemical Inventor as a career popped into my head, but I pushed it away, because studying glue would get boring.

Ruby and I told the story of how we constructed the treehouse last summer while my parents were getting divorced.

I added in about how my dad used to punch my mom where the bruises wouldn't show, and how the police cars took up all the guest parking in the trailer park whenever I used my pay-as-you-go to call 911.

You need to always have at least five minutes remaining on your phone just to be safe, because the switchboard can put you on hold if it's a busy crime night.

Like on full moons, I've noticed.

I tried to detect if the information about my dad compared to the situation Blake was in with his dad. Except there was one critical difference—my own dad never hit me. I think I'm more around the level of furniture to him, or maybe at the same level as Wiener our wiener dog, who gets fed but never petted, except by me.

I even gave Wiener a spa treatment in the bathtub once with lavender dog soap, but he shivered in fear and I felt bad.

Anyway, Blake and Albert didn't show any signs of being abused kids, or give off any clues or secret sideways glances—they just looked normal.

But Blake was the one covering up bruises with his clothing—I would bet all my quarters because my real mom Cheryl used to cover her bruises, too.

"Aren't you allowed to have a cell phone?" I asked.

Blake shook his head. "Negatory on the texting thing for me. Mom won't pay for it."

I thought for a moment and then I said, "why don't you try my phone," and I reached into my shorts pocket and tossed the Nokia.

Time went into slow motion for me as my phone tumbled through the air, flashing silver and black, like the scales of a fish underwater that's about to dart under a rock.

The eighties song *She's A Maniac* popped into my head.

Blake caught the phone and instantly tossed it back. "Thanks, but no thanks," he said. "My mom would skin me if she found it."

Ruby moved us on to other topics, such as how Blake and Albert would be honorary members of our justice club, and how we scout the neighborhood looking for crimes to document and we hoped they would join us.

Our good works include, but are not limited to: Collecting by hand all the highway trash in the drainage ditch once a month to protect the egret that lives there with its very long freaky beak. Going to the grocery store for Mrs. Wilbers when she broke her hip. And helping Billy paint his white wooden fence again really quickly when an artist hoodlum spray-painted a man's butt bending over across the boards. It was very realistic.

I'm not kidding.

I felt like I got an education.

Blake and Albert and Ruby and I got on swimmingly that afternoon. Ruby did manage to ask Blake about the injury on his palm. And Blake did manage to explain it was from falling off his skateboard.

Ruby and I exchanged knowing looks.

We both know sometimes the situation gets worse when you tell the truth.

I just felt like there was something so familiar about Blake. I kept thinking about his face being twisted, his pale lips bared back in a grimace of desperation.

That I'd seen that same look before on someone else.

Well, I was starting to feel really bad that my legs had froze up under the RV. Like there Blake was getting beat up in the shed with a belt, and I had turned all cowardly.

I just needed to know something more.

We're not an all-talk-no-action group.

I knew what I had to do. And I hoped Ruby would understand I had to do it alone.

AT JUST PAST MIDNIGHT THAT NIGHT MY DAD AND STEP-NOT-mom were still watching some kind of police show on the couch.

I snuck outside in the cloak of darkness. I knew they'd never notice I was missing. I'm as invisible as Wiener.

I rode my bike to Safeway and the cashier helped me count all the quarters, even though they were pre-counted. I bought a big piece of middle-class meat. I pedaled my bike in the inky dark down Old Buttermilk Lane until I was at the hulking shadow of the RV.

There were like zero cars. Or people. Plenty of yellow porch lights on dark slumbering stoops, and some TV lights flashing behind the private curtains of bedroom windows.

I hid my bike in the shadows.

The air smelled faintly like skunk.

My heart kinda started beating harder, like Band-Aids were wrapped around it and squeezing.

I tiptoed up to Blake's chain-link fence and plopped the meat onto the cement on the other side. It just laid there dead. If that Chihuahua came running out it was going to have too much steak in its mouth to bark.

I climbed over the chain-link fence.

It rattled and I thought of rattlesnakes coiled up in the dark.

The shed door loomed up ahead. I couldn't take it anymore, the shadows were growing arms and my neck hairs were freaking out so I risked turning on the flashlight of my Nokia.

But sometimes a little bit of light just makes things worse and I ended up in a brief *Star Wars* scene where my phone was a light saber and I slashed it in every direction.

I got myself under control.

I tiptoed up to the shed door, the cold knob turned in

my shaking hand, and I slipped into the enclosure quiet as a mouse.

Except for the huge box of miscellaneous engine odds and ends that I knocked down with a clatter. This is why Ruby is going to be the movie star and I'm backstage.

After realizing that I did not pee my pants, and also after a full five minutes remaining frozen in a crouched position, squeezing my Nokia with a death latch, I finally decided Mr. Beefy must still be asleep and I stood up and began hunting.

Rows of gunmetal shelves towered over me.

Dusty boxes and cobwebs and decades of junk built up everywhere my flashlight glowed. A decapitated doll's head. A cracked football helmet. A black mannequin without arms.

The back of my throat tasted like mold.

I had no idea which corner to turn.

Then I had the idea to shine my light on the ground and like a sprinkle of magic fairy dust a worn path shone in gray footprints, a tattle-teller in the grime.

The footprints led to the back of the rectangular shed. There was a filthy mattress there. Handcuffs hanging on a pole. And after searching more, I saw the professional camera on the tripod.

And I found the laptop and the pile of disks.

Bingo, I thought, because I'd seen this abuse setup on an Oprah show. Then I got the hell out of there.

That middle-class meat was still laying dead on the ground.

I NEEDED A FEW DAYS BY MYSELF TO THINK. I TOLD RUBY I had the flu.

Maybe another person would have called the authorities already.

All I know is that the last time I called the police to get my dad arrested for trying to kill my mom, they arrested my mom instead.

She's in a federal prison in Kansas now for attempted murder. We write letters every week. I guess the honest testimony of a seven-year-old child didn't mean anything to the law.

My mom is innocent. My mom was defending herself. I watched it happen. I will never forget her face how it twisted, her pale lips bared back in a grimace of desperation.

I will never forget his lies.

And my dad's a bit of an evil genius. I give him that. I hope it's worn off on me—but in the opposite direction.

You know, so like I can become a super good person, instead.

I spend a lot of nights sleeping in the Infamous Technotronic Treehouse to be away from him. He disgusts me. That's the real reason we built it, and put in a sleeping bag, but Ruby promised she'd never tell anyone.

My so-called room in our trailer house is just the couch, anyway. I'm allowed to keep my clean clothes under the bathroom sink.

Ruby is amazing because she hides presents for me.

And written notes tucked inside my sleeping bag like an old-fashioned text message.

There's often a useful reminder: Felicia, in the morning don't freak out and think the egret is an alien again.

And the note's always signed: Your Best Friend Forever, Ruby.

I know she limits her texts and calls to me so I have all my cell minutes just in case I get scared out here, you know?

But I'll never call 911 again.

I mean, wait. I would need to call them just one more time. But not now. Not yet. There was a little organization to do.

AFTER TWO DAYS OF THE NOT-FLU I GATHERED ALL FOUR OF US at the Infamous Technotronic Treehouse.

If we were going to be an official justice club, we needed an official name. Secondly, we needed some ground rules for the summer, or a code of conduct, to pin to the wall. And a way to keep track of our justice projects. If other kids wanted to join when the word got out, I was okay with that.

And lastly, we had to agree to support each other. No matter what happened. Like if one of us had to testify in court or something. Ruby shot me a look with that one.

It was Blake who suggested The Ball Breaker's Summer Club.

I like that kid.

When I called the police on Mr. Beefy, I made sure it was dark and misty and I was alone. I hid under the RV. I took a lot of deep breaths until I thought I might pass out from hyperventilation, and then I decided enough already.

Just do it.

Wait, it's called a recreational vehicle. My body flooded with relief like a bad itch was suddenly gone.

I dialed 911 and I started screaming bloody murder. I said I was being held hostage in handcuffs in the shed. I gave the address. I saw lights coming on as neighbors looked around for what bad thing was happening.

Then I crawled out the back of the RV and disappeared into the mist.

I saw the red-and-blue flashers as I sailed down Old Buttermilk Lane on my bike. I had already crushed my cell phone and threw it in the blackberry bushes. I think pay-as-you-go is untraceable, but not if you're still carrying it around.

Anyway, sometimes justice means just us.

I'm not saying what I did was right. I'm just saying it's what I did. I've learned in this world we have to decide for ourselves where the line is between good and bad.

I've drawn where I stand.

MOTHER ROCK MAMBA

DWYN'S HIDE-BANDAGED ankle made her snake boot drag in the desert sands.

The leather toe was damaged, pulled off the sole so the top bent backward on a crease like a mouth—and when she swung her leg, the mouth opened and flashed her toes like a row of dirty teeth.

Each step caused a spike of pain.

Sometimes she got a faint whiff of a rotting cabbage stink from her foot.

She didn't dare tell.

The others thought she was limping because her shoe was broken. And because Dwyn was small and weak like a runt. But her mouth tasted sickly sweet, like those puffy things called Twinkie. And a line of bad sweat was beading on her upper lip.

The dunes floated into the unending horizon, brown sands mixed with strange, charred rubble; and Dwyn's tribe of eight weary people lumbered toward the sunken skyscraper city. The skinny, wild eyed and hungry dog pack followed behind.

The dogs weren't loyal or anything: They followed for the human waste. It was all they had to eat, because dogs don't use can openers.

The sound of everyone's feet; that's what you heard.

Wshh-wshh, constant across the sands.

No one spoke.

Sunbaked concrete monsters in the distance pillared out of the earth and leaned sideways like colossal sand worms, rusted steel marrow spilling out of their strange cracked bones.

The buried city of Lost Angels was only a few hours walk. A few hours until they could touch the bones. Dream big city dreams of food and needed things from the past.

The orange sun.

Always a fireball burning a hole through tormented clouds, chemical mushrooms billowing up with a ghostly purple flange—and beyond the clouds it looked like a mad giant had took a hammer and pounded the whole copper sheet of sky.

Pretty colors up there, if death was pretty.

Especially at sunset when the sun made oily rainbows shimmer and dance, before all the light fell west, and the earth, "our mother rock", got suffocated in an abyss of black. Black as a cave, until the gray touch of sun peeked back up in the east.

You always felt relief when the dirty dawn came, and you could see the charcoal outlines of your own disembodied hands again where you lay.

Like your own hands were coming down to squeeze your face hello.

Dwyn never saw any stars her whole sixteen winters of life.

Old Uncle said they'd used to been like twinkling diamonds, an array of alien worlds; then he'd hold up his hands like he was the old-fashioned sky itself, and on each stubby finger was a glittering diamond ring winking in the sun—just look at these beauties, he'd say. Just like real starlight. His eyes would get that crazy far-away look, and his crooked smile showed black rotted teeth.

Not stars, whatever stars really looked like; just useless clear rocks.

They made Uncle have a constant bloody scab, because when he went to wipe the nasal drip, the rocks cut his nose.

And that day when his hand got bit by a black sand snake, no one could pull the big rings off for the swelling, and his skin all around burst, just like how the skin sloughs off stewed tomatoes—those kind from the bigger sized cans. Then Mother had to machete Uncle's hand off to save him, because she was the decider of those things; and he died right then, anyway. From the snake bite, how it freezes your heart.

The tribe didn't eat their own meat.

Didn't bury it, either. Fed it to the dogs.

So Dwyn had thought about this when Mother gave her tripe that night.

And Dwyn accepted her share of dog stew in the bowl,

but snuck off and buried it all just before blackout. And prayed for Uncle and said thanks.

Uncle had been strange and crazy, but he was good.

Uncle had taught Dwyn about books, when no one was watching. Taught her how to read. How to use a divining rod for water. How to file steel. They'd had a learning secret.

Uncle told stories of when they had started walking from a place called Baja. Everyone was crazier then, he said. That was before Dwyn was born—somewhere—and Uncle said her brain had less toxins than everybody else.

She asked about Baja.

What was new? It was always sand.

But the air changed here, a few weeks ago.

Dwyn remembered the first time it smelled like someone else's sweaty armpit. Salty, rotten. That was really how to describe it—and Dwyn had thought on it a lot. If the sky smelled like your *own* armpit, that'd be good, you'd get to trust it.

But this new smell was a suspicious stranger.

The kind that stabbed you in the back if you got comfortable.

Sometimes the wind blew a peppermint gift. It cleared your dusty sinuses like a shot of firewater at first, but after awhile it burned right through and made your nose bleed. And you didn't even get drunk and laughy. You just got sick.

So you learned there were no gifts from the sky here.

Just staying together with your own tribe. And finding supplies, trading with friendlies.

Dwyn wanted to go north were it was rumored there was green land.

The mythical color of green.

But none of the tribe believed in green.

Dwyn sneezed. A long thing of brown snot hung off her nose. She wiped it with the side of her leather glove on her right hand. That's why she wore a single glove. For the nasal drip.

Other's just let it hang and go where it went.

She felt her ankle pain getting worse. Maybe they were just an hour away now. Her blue tarp backpack started cutting into her shoulders, getting heavier and heavier for no reason.

Everyone walking. No one talking. The sun beating down like that mad giant's hammer.

With those mushroom clouds billowing, Dwyn knew rain might come, but it would be taking its good and toxic time to fall because rain hardly fell down anymore. You were lucky to find water in bottles in the cities buried underground, but unlucky if water fell from heaven.

Heaven hated the people.

All the people should have all died all over Earth, but nah; not everyone did. Dwyn didn't even know what had happened to the ruined cities, what had caused the deserts to swallow the world.

No one did.

Maybe the sky should forgive them already.

One time Dwyn saw a single raindrop bore through the leg of a good, fresh cut of dog meat; sizzle it right down to the white bone, and sizzle right through that and the black iron pan, too. Gave off a thin yellow smoke.

They all ran underground to a buried thing called a parking garage, while the downpour ate their food all by itself. These things called automobiles were heaps of fine sand, all lined up in perfect rows, but if you dug into a pile, you could sometimes find sharp metal edges, and could file them sharper, to carry in your sleeve.

The chemical sky had an eye to surprise you.

When anyone in the tribe got caught in a rain pour, you didn't go back for them.

You never went back. That was good respect not to go see the acid bore holes so their faces had twenty new eyes and their brains were looking out.

Beads of feverish sweat started to sting Dwyn's eyes, even with the dog hide scarf wrapped around her head to protect her face from the constant sun—she glanced back at her tracks, how far she had come, and turning her head made her dizzy.

Her limping snake boot trail looked like it was made of that lost English language, their old number eight.

Two suns on top each other.

It was a friendly number, nice to draw; but nobody wrote stuff anymore—except Dwyn.

It was important to remember everything front and center in your mind. And the tribe said when you wrote stuff down, you just gave yourself permission to *forget* it.

Like a dictionary. Isn't that crazy? They used to have a million words they didn't even need and don't even know what they mean.

Nobody wrote nothing now.

They had it all memorized. How to make fire, how to build a sandstorm shelter, how to lash a tarp to your back, folded in a triangle so no fine sand could sneak in. How to cut up the dogs. Identify the edible parasites.

The color of charcoal that makes the safest face filter, when you dig just under the top layers of sand.

How to tap a tin can and know what was for dinner. (Dwyn never once, never *ever,* had got this right. She'd say chili bean and it'd be black olives. She'd say olives and it'd be corn.)

The pain in her ankle got sharper.

Her tongue had lost the sickly Twinkie taste—it was dry and flaky now. Getting dryer.

> Twinkie: n.
>
> trademark snack food, supposedly invented in 1930 by Jimmy Dewar, baker for Continental Baking Co.

Dwyn always wondered about Jimmy, if he'd been a prophet. He'd made the only thing left on earth that the acid rain couldn't eat. It just rolled off.

The sun pounded down on Dwyn's head, making her vision taper on the edges. This wasn't good. Getting dizzier.

She should tell someone, but you didn't want to tell no one your secrets. You didn't want to become dog food, just in case.

The tribe chose for the survival of the tribe. The decider chose. They all understood the rules.

After a month of walking, their packs were too light, the cans were gone, water low. They needed the Lost Angel's city now. Right now. Before everyone dehydrated and fell.

And the dogs got fat.

But when Dwyn smacked her face on the sand, her vision fading all the way to dark, her last thought was that this secret—the accidental gash on her foot—would be known.

WHEN DWYN WOKE UP NAKED AND LYING IN THE SAND, everything was blue.

Disoriented, she jerked her head up; and sand rained out of her knotted, long hair with a tinkling sensation across her cheeks, the bridge of her nose.

Her lips were glued together. Her tongue was gone. No, the tongue was just glued to the roof of her mouth like a solid piece.

She opened her mouth wide like a yawn and her tongue tore off her palate.

Then, there was blood in her mouth.

A plastic water bottle sat buried halfway in sand before her nose, cast under the same blue light. The label was all rubbed off, but for the vertical letters PURI, and Dwyn knew it was her own bottle, cause she'd only sipped the last of her water down to the R.

And now it was filled with hard yellow piss. No cap. The piss smell hit Dwyn.

The blue color: Her tarp backpack, unfolded over her whole body like a blanket. Dwyn jerked up onto an elbow and cast the tarp off.

The fireball sun hammered nails into her eyes. The gray-brown desert lengthened in every direction, larger and more monstrous than ever before.

And eerie quiet.

Dwyn thought her ears went deaf, but then she heard the sound of her own labored breathing. They'd left her covered up in her own tarp. Oh no. They'd *left* her.

She knew how it would have went down: When she fainted, they'd tried to revive her. Probably slapped her face. Untied her boot to investigate her limp, found her wound filled with pus. Infected.

She was dead weight right then.

The tribe'd been twenty long faces a month ago, and—

Seven now—stumbling onward to the next set of underground ruins, an hour away. An hour—or *never*.

Obviously no one had volunteered to carry her.

So they'd distributed Dwyn's stuff. Drank her water. And somebody'd done the piss thing, pissed all over her injury to mask the smell of rotting flesh, soaked the piss deep into her leather boot—so the wild dogs would loose interest, and keep following the tribe's scent, like the tribe needed them to do.

Dwyn clenched her hands into fists. Just because she was little, and invisible, and had never learned to fight. And wanted to learn lost languages.

And collect dictionaries.

Well, at least Mother didn't machete her up.

And pack her skinny parts for dog food. There must have been enough of Uncle still left in the travois. Dwyn chewed her lip. Then a smile flickered on her face.

His meaty limbs had saved her life.

"Don't worry." She reached up to her neck and found the chipped diamond ring she wore on a leather cord and gave it a gentle squeeze. It was sharp. "Nobody wanted this."

But that smile fell fast when she saw a dark line rippling to the east. Undulating, back and forth, back and forth; slowly getting bigger.

A black snake.

A damned big mean black snake, sailing across the dunes, right at her.

Adrenaline spiked her chest.

viper: n.

a. venomous snake with large hinged fangs, typically having a broad head and stout body, deadly

b. malignant or spiteful person

Dwyn's teeth snapped shut.

Got to her hands and knees. Her heartbeat thudding in her neck.

The tribe had abandoned her, the adults with weapons gone, and Dwyn was naked all over, just wearing boots. She stood. She ran a step, pain shot up to her knee. She fell hard.

Sand sprayed her eyes.

The sun burned her skin.

She rose to her feet, the ankle rolled again. She fell on her ribs.

That snake got bigger, flying over the sand. Whipping its long body, back and forth, back and forth.

"No," Dwyn screamed. But it was just a hoarse scratch in her throat. Blood sprayed from her lips where the roof of her mouth was torn.

The snake wanted her because it was smarter than a dog.

It could smell the weakness underneath the piss.

Dwyn lost her muscles, they went wimpy like noodles. Those long Cup 'O Noodles that nobody could digest. She dragged herself backward on her butt, with useless legs, sand filling her boots at the ankles, dragging weight.

The huge black snake slowed at the far edge of the blue tarp, nosed it; languid, liquid. It looked like a piece of the blackest part of midnight, like a fissure in the sand that could open and open more until she fell through.

Dwyn's stomach muscles squeezed the pee out of her own guts.

That pink forked tongue flicked and flicked: Judging her. Cold, predator eyes. The sleek, scaly black body coiled a little; neck up, head down. Just enough.

It struck.

Dwyn's legs kicked, a lightening strike in primordial defense. The snake's fangs bit the broken flap on her boot.

The fangs got stuck there.

This time the scream coming out of Dwyn's throat grew

louder and louder, an inhuman wail vibrating out of her lungs, as her body entwined with the whip and writhe of the black muscled viper and they rolled together violently down a sand dune.

The snake's angry snake fangs still caught in the boot flap.

Dwyn's terrified hands wringing its powerful, twisting neck.

Until they stopped rolling, and Dwyn ripped the chipped diamond ring from her neck and slit the snake's throat open.

A gush of hot blood squirted over her hands, bubbling up, frothy and splashing her face.

The snake body slapped her; flipped sideways, creamy underbelly. Then flipped back to black—fangs still caught in the boot. Body still twisting this way and that: But weaker now.

Weaker.

And Dwyn sobbed.

Salty tears rained her lips.

She unwound the snake, scooted backward on her butt again. The dead serpent stretched into a long, impossibly long, straight line. The sunlight winked silver off its reptilian scales.

Its deadly fangs were *still* hopelessly jammed in the boot flap. Dwyn's boot wouldn't wiggle off her ankle.

And it was as if they were connected forever now.

This balance between dead and not dead.

She breathed like that; shallow, just in shock. Her skin vibrated. The sunlight changed: It reached a hand down, stroking each knobby vertebrae on her back, and the heat embraced her like a kindly human might, if anyone had ever kindly touched her.

She didn't really want to die out here.

So she scooched forward and cut off the rest of the head. And carefully pried off the freaky fang mouth and heaved it away.

Thunk.

The adults in the tribe had skinned things. Dwyn had seen it a million times. So she peeled the snake with the chipped diamond ring, and only gagged once when she nicked the stomach and it exploded.

The shimmering skin lay in a pile to her right, stinking. The lump of guts lay in a pile to her left, stinking more. Her legs were streaked with slime, and in some places, it had already dried like strange, foreign tattoos.

She made herself eat some meat for strength.

Chew. Swallow. Chew. Swallow. Done.

She investigated her hide-bandage, pulled out the charcoal pieces that she'd pressed into the painful, infected wound. The dictionary definition of charcoal was that it can *absorb,* but it had taken days until the tribe had found and burned some wood.

Dwyn had treated her cut in secret yesterday.

But maybe the chunks needed to be a powder? A paste?

She grated the charcoal together into a thick dust, packed her gash, retied the hide bandage, then wrapped the snake skin into a strong brace. Tied it just below her knee. Now she had one black leg with shiny, silver glints.

The sun sank even lower into the afternoon—getting ready to play its game of hide-and-seek. *Follow me, find me.*

Dwyn crawled on hands and knees back up the sand dune; drank urine to hydrate, refolded her backpack. The world was silent. A rare insect flew by, buzzing. Gone. Only then did she dare to try standing on the brace; both afraid to succeed, and afraid to fail. She succeeded.

She'd never been alone before in her whole life.

It was a bad dream come true.

Golden rays silhouetted the colossal ruins up ahead, and now that she looked, the fossilized remains of the mysterious past seemed more like a dark gray forest of concrete skeletons.

Did the tribe make it there?

Would they accept her back?

Seven people's deep, empty footprints led a path into the vanishing horizon, pockmarked by paws.

She set off in their wake, naked—into the fiery orange and red skyline, and then turned and came back for the snake head. The evil eyes were sunken in, opaque. It still freaked her out, but she might need it for the dogs. She put it in her pack.

Limping. Stumbling. Falling, getting up. Her arms felt the brush strokes of air getting cooler, the hairs on her arms sensitive like raw nerves. Except for the parts of her body insulated in guts and adhered sand, which had dried into a hard paste.

Maybe she was part snake, now.

It would be easier to slither, than to walk. Easier to be the predator, than the prey. Nothing came easy.

She listened to the lone sound of her own feet whistle against the sand. *Wshh-sh. Wshh-sh.*

In all her travels, sometimes the sand itself was naked, and sometimes it had rubble strewn everywhere; or it rose and fell like small mountains, or shimmered like a waterless lake. But right now the placid expanse of sand had only one unusual shape as she approached it from afar—aside from seven sets of human footprints. A suspicious rectangular lump. It fluttered, like a broken wing.

Her pocket dictionary.

No one else could read English. So English got tossed.

Dwyn stopped at the edge of the tattered book. Nudged it with her boot. Why did it seem like a trap?

She bent to fold the pages carefully back into the broken spine just so, and some beloved pages were missing. Dwyn scanned the area, looking for the M's section—as if those words had all mutinied, jumped the page and scurried away like tiny rats, and the blank pages themselves had given chase.

But nothing moved, except the dark shadows lengthening from the towering ruins; maybe only ten minutes away.

Now it was becoming night.

The hair prickled on Dwyn's neck.

A figure darted into the shadows up ahead, darted behind the concrete structure. A human figure. She'd seen half a shoulder, a head. Was it a real person? She dropped to the still-warm sand fast, it scratched her belly. Just like when she would hide behind Uncle when he said: Stay, wait.

Except Uncle carried sharp spears, and they could soar.

Dwyn needed a spear.

Through the layers of shadow, intertwining and becoming the void of nightfall, another thing moved with shoulders and a head.

Dwyn wiggled out of her pack, slowly reaching inside along the crunchy material, bypassing the piss-bottle with a snakeskin stopper, bypassing a handful of spongy raw meat cubes.

Her fingers throbbed with fear; if that snake head had tricked her, if it had come back alive. But Dwyn's finger poked its soft eye, and squished it.

She slipped her hand backward through the snake mouth, carefully lodging her fingers away from the venom sacs—exactly like a puppet.

puppet: n.

a. movable model of person or animal, typically controlled by strings from above or a hand inside it

b. a person, party, or state under the control of another person, group, or power

The sun died and the starless abyss ate Dwyn up for dinner like it always did.

She emptied the piss in a circle around her body, marking her territory.

She lay coiled all night.

Listening and listening.

And even when she slept, her hand lay ready to bite.

DAWN BROKE UGLY.

The ashen ruins emerged from dark, at first a charcoal sketch, and then the sun colored yellow a hundred rows of hollow eyes, the skyscrapers rising up over Dywns head, windblown shells filled with mounds of tawny sand—the vampires of memory having sucked pale the pages of this civilization's history and left only the title on the broken spine.

The End.

The question was *why*. And even more perplexing: How come the tribe didn't want to know? They wandered the vast sands, plundering its dwindling riches like ghosts. And Uncle had said: Memories are splinters and they want them all pulled.

But for Dwyn—memories were seeds. And they needed to be put where things could grow.

The sunlight warmed her back.

She eyed her snake hand, and her heart fluttered a bit, just to visually see the predator—but it also seemed like a comfort, to have a fang defense.

No strange figures stood in the light, and the ruins seemed vacant, but for the continuing trail of seven sets of footprints from yesterday, but no paws following, not now. The dog pack had held off at the ridge behind Dwyn and headed south.

Maybe they'd seen the figure—smelled something wrong.

Dwyn stood up. Her snake brace had dried more;

stiffer, stronger. She took a few cautious steps. The charcoal powder must be working, pressed up against her skin. Absorbing. Maybe she'd outsmarted infection, something that had never been outsmarted before.

The concept of medicine.

She stood in the echoes of her tribe's prints and touched the pale gray, pitted and pockmarked surface of the first wall.

Red flakes of rust showered and coated the back of her hand.

It's like a metaphor, she thought. The dried blood of the lost people.

And maybe this was where Mother's palm had touched, flesh to stone. So they would have pressed onward, looking for an entrance in and down.

Dwyn followed, walking among giants.

All the footprints converged into a narrow track, and the fireball sun's rays got blocked out by the giants, and Dwyn entered a labyrinth. Orange-tinted shadows and crumbling walls, and up above; huge sections balanced deadly on thin air.

Waiting for a breath to make it all collapse.

Like just the buzz of tiny wings.

And this felt even more like a trap, and that feeling might be the definition of intuition. So Dwyn stopped. She was being funneled into a choke point. She looked up, again. And this time she saw something beside ruins. She saw something strange.

A dangling rope hanging out of a window. The rope

was frayed. And she could see the line where it could have been hidden, before it was freed.

The air started tasting like peppermint; that deadly peppermint chemical that sometimes blew from nowhere.

Dwyn raised her snake puppet up toward the rope; if she could flick the snake tongue and have snake senses, what weakness would she find here?

Then, she looked down at the sand, and on either of the sides where no footprints tread, a new thing had left tracks. A grid.

A net.

To catch people.

It had been hidden under the sand.

One by one as they walked yesterday, her tribe had been snared, and jerked up in a net. Yes, up ahead, before the narrow path twisted around a corner, another frayed rope dangled.

She recognized the trap, because the word trap was both a noun and a verb, and had thirteen definitions, and drawings, too.

The peppermint wind thickened, irritating Dwyn's nose. She didn't have time to run back. She needed to get underground, find a crevasse, a crawl hole—to get away from the chemical.

She hesitated.

She removed the fang puppet and stowed it in her pack —threw a blob of meat down her throat. Somehow, it tasted like cold cream of corn soup.

The first foothold crumbled when the toe of her boot

dug in. The second foothold crumbled, too. The peppermint air kept thickening.

Soon her nose would bleed and not stop bleeding.

She untied her boots, stuffed them into the pack, climbed up with her wiry fingers and toes—her malnourished body light as a feather; until the rope grazed her side as if it might sprout a head and bite her naked ribs, and then she lost concentration and almost fell.

Over the lip of the steel window ledge, and the rope was tied to a makeshift anchor out of heavy rocks in the center of a large room.

Yellow sunlight dazzled the walls, where strange objects dangled, wires and tentacles. On the ceiling, these things they had called fluorescents that held firelight for reading. Every object was mysterious, its purpose unknown to her.

One set of human tracks, the lookout. She bet he was afraid of snakes.

And this person had a missing toe.

Dwyn slunk down sandy, steel-beam stairs, following where the enemy had went. She could see down through holes in the steps, down toward what would be death if she fell.

The chemical peppermint faded away, and an earthy musk funneled up from underground.

A hint of smoke.

The sounds of her own feet shuffling.

Down and down she wound until she sank past the ground level of the building, and the sunlit stairs got dimmer, and dimmer; until everything went back to being painted in gray tones like the predawn. She felt like she'd entered a tomb.

The air got cold, damp.

The weight of the world was above.

She thought about how when all the cans in the ruins ran out, or rusted—if they ate the dogs and the dogs ate them, then they would eat each other out of existence.

That's what had been bothering her for a long time. A sense of urgency. A sense of needing to find people who wanted to remember the past. And learn of the ancients, and plant seeds where it was green.

What if they were supposed to rebuild it? The world that had come before?

A new smell hit her, the smell of a familiar armpit. All of their armpits.

Then a smile flickered on her face.

"Hello?" she whispered.

No reply.

She let her nose lead her down what had been a hallway until seven bodies lay bound and gagged in what had been a room.

Mother saw her first, and she must have thought she'd seen a ghost. She closed her eyes.

Ah yes, Dwyn thought. I'm unusually naked.

Dwyn took off her chipped diamond and cut through the ropes that bound them all, and quickly they gave her back her hides and she dressed.

They spoke to her excitedly in hushed tones, and slapped her on her back many times until her teeth rattled, and pointed to her snake leg, because she had saved them, look at that! And told her she was an adult now, wasn't she? Good work, Runt! Come with us, let's get the cannibals. Let's take this place, we can stay here.

Whatever this place was, it wasn't worth taking.

And Mother squeezed her hand tight; then let go.

When the tribe gathered to make an attack plan, then headed down the hallway deeper into the underground, Dwyn took up the rear. They really thought she was coming with them.

And then she stopped walking.

She just stopped. And they disappeared.

She retraced her way back to the stairs, back up into the warm, yellow sunlight, carefully sniffing the air to determine the peppermint chemical that blew randomly out of the sky was gone, back into the room with the frayed rope.

She held onto the rope's end, dropped to the ground, saw a loose piece of steel rebar and picked it up, running out from the giant's tombs. Back to the circle of pee—which was dry, of course. And the pocket dictionary, which she felt horrified she had forgotten to put in her backpack.

It had waited for her. Knowing she would come back.

All her life, never being alone, never *on* her own; and now it was all she wanted. Almost.

fate: v.

to be destine to happen, turn out, or act in a particular way

She walked back up the ridge and found the dog prints,

followed them. She pulled the last of the snake meat out and held it in her hand. The sun went all the way to straight up overhead by the time a dog finally raised its head over a dune and came near.

She fastened the black snake head to the metal pole.

The dogs eyed her. Later she would file it into a spear. She would gather more charcoal and make a mask filter for the peppermint air. And more wound medicine. And do Uncle's divining rod for water.

I'm a snake hunter now.

Dwyn left the meat on the sand.

Walked a little bit away. Left more meat.

The first dog followed. Then another.

Up north was the promised green land.

THE CHICKEN TIME MACHINE

LABCORP TECHNICIAN #34, old man Mr. Dungaree, pedaled the rickety bicycle along the rainy, miserable side of Highway 101, as fast as his short legs, and the even shorter allowance of the stitched inseam to his soaking wet cotton pants, would allow.

So all in all, this was terribly slow.

Plus, he had a near paralytic fear of bicycle contraptions.

And cars kept whizzing by, spitting foam and debris into his chapped red face. Cold water stung his eyes and blurred his vision. The air smelled just like Pine Forest scented lab toilet cleaner. The black garbage-bag jacket that he had so carefully duct-taped together to make sleeves, suddenly ripped apart at the seams, cold water pouring down his neck as it fluttered behind him like a failed parachute.

Cardinal rule: Don't Attract Attention.

Well, screw all the fools' rules.

When his wobbly front tire hit potholes it made his teeth snap shut like a shark. For which he had already twice paid the price for mouth-breathing, and bit his tongue like a self-eating madman—and suffered the uncourteous swallow of his own rusty-tasting blood.

Too much ferrous oxide in this most vital fluid.

Dangerous levels.

The broken seat springs went *chrricka-chrricka,* threatening to crumple away and expose a potentially impaling metal post—and this made the unmistakable entrance to Mr. Dungaree's internal organs cringe.

The autumn rain storm, along the northern coast of the Pacific landmass of what was still considered California, had gone utterly insane.

Or maybe *real* weather had always been like this—how would he know?

Unabashedly liquid.

Mr. Dungaree wanted to holler into his lapel Tele, *Turn the showers down, you dolt!,* but LabCorp UB12 was now, oh —a mere two hundred years into the future, and telepathic technology didn't even exist yet.

Mr. Dungaree was the dolt now.

And all for the love of *eggs.*

He could kick himself in the pants if his own pants and the broken seat of this stolen bicycle weren't kicking him there enough already. How had he managed this time machine blunder? No self-respecting scientist would have made the mistake.

But then, of course, having time-machined backward into the strange year 2017—and appeared here naked (*ahem*), homeless, broke, and having to resort to thievery—he was fresh out of self-respect.

He was flush with stupidity, however.

Could build an empire with his stupidity. If empires could be built that way. Oh wait, that's right, empires *had* been built on stupidity; and that's why the whole Earth had an apocalypse and they'd all been underground for forty years, and would be for at least a hundred more.

Kinda like Noah's ark but they didn't all get happily along. And there weren't two of each.

Because right now, if Mr. Dungaree had a double copy of himself back in LabCorp UB12, he'd go ahead and steer this version into traffic straight away.

The brake lights of a truck flashed red, steering off the highway and down the off-ramp to the little town of Trinidad. Mr. Dungaree followed, his arms beginning to shake in earnest with cold, griping the handlebars with white knuckles.

Chrricka-chrricka, the seat laughed.

Then Mr. Dungaree's teeth started to chatter like chipmunks. And just about the time he had a swell of hope that he could coast this terrible, evil bicycle to a full stop, he lost his balance and toppled sideways into an oily mud puddle anyway.

Now he was not only homeless, broke, and starving—but dirty as a hog, too. Mr. Dungaree immediately patted his chest, seeking confirmation of the final coil of copper wire in his flannel shirt he'd just illegally cut out of a nearby substation, as well as the wire cutters used to commit this particular crime.

Thank heavens.

Rain pinged off the top of his head, irritating his sensitive bald crown, which had not received its customary comb-over for the entire month he'd been zapped into the god-forsaken past.

Mr. Dungaree then had the bright idea to salvage the garbage bag, with a makeshift umbrella in mind, but he got in a fight with the plastic as it gusted in the wind and suctioned over his face.

Diesel grit coated his lips and stung his eyes.

After a string of futuristic expletives, Mr. Dungaree left the trash bag and the bicycle laying together to die in treachery.

He had two of his own legs, and they still worked —thank you.

The fluffy pink female slippers he wore squished with mud as he hobbled across the street toward the gas station lit up in bright signs. Actually, the slippers were no longer a shade of pink. Nor resembling slippers.

But he wore them because all the undergrounders had weak arches as sensitive as a baby's butt. That's what you get for walking up and down smooth, flat ramps your whole life.

He reached the shelter of the gas pump roof and pulled out a handful of brown paper towels from the self-service rack—gently daubed his face, and avoided a few sideways glances with the two paying customers barbarically wasting fuel in their prehistoric machines.

Idiots.

However, they did seem just as equally unimpressed with him. So it was mutual.

Mr. Dungaree's whole body then decided to convulse as if he were actually buried in snow instead of manageably rain soaked, and thusly he decided it was indeed an emergency, and he would need to risk entry into the establishment for a dry-off.

The fingerprint-smudged glass door opened with a cheery *ding-dong!*, warm air brushed his cheeks, and Mr. Dungaree slopped across the tiled floor in a rush for the bathroom, hoping the cashier would not notice.

The cashier noticed.

But it was that redheaded surfer fellow and he was more humanitarian, than, shall we say: *It's the strict policy of the establishment, Sir.*

Then the waft of scrambled eggs from the hot plate buffet hit Mr. Dungaree. He went weak in the knees as he shuffled past.

The supplier was the restaurant Mama's Pig 'N Pancake. (Come in, we care). The kindly chef was the renowned Mama Jane Paganelli.

Buttery bliss, savory earth, and a mildly rich and creamy undertone. A moist, spongy texture, with an ever-so-light spring back—and the more Mama marvelously whisked the eggs, the fluffier they would become.

Cheesy, salt-and peppered, sensual heaven.

Light and delicate with a down-home, bless-the-morning, footie-pajamas-type charm.

But the true secret was the addition of a splash of

pancake batter. Yes! She did! Pancake batter in the egg bowl.

Oh indeed, that's right, it was ten a.m. on a weekday and my goodness there were egg remnants still left uneaten in the silver tray.

Wasteful blasphemy!

Mr. Dungaree's eyes fluttered closed for a moment; and it was all he could do to control his numb fingers which twitched, and his diesel-tasting mouth, which madly salivated for revival.

He almost attacked the hot plate like a werewolf (or a nearly hairless werewolf, at least).

Who cared about the other two trays—the crisp bacon, the single slice left of sweet French toast—it was all about *real* eggs.

(Well, not that Mr. Dungaree wouldn't have eaten sautéed cardboard right about *now* to quell his starvation. He was just making a culinary point.)

Mr. Dungaree nearly wept as the egg aroma faded.

He widened his nostrils and inhaled like a desperate man.

The nearing restrooms overpowered the delightful aroma with toilet stench. When Mr. Dungaree opened the men's door, a waft of urine rose up like an olfactory tidal wave and consumed him with the misery of his homelessness, his timelessness—his utter scientific ineptitude.

But the final copper wires poked through the pocket in his dirty flannel shirt.

And all hope was not yet lost.

Not yet.

At least the hot water streaming from the public sink was indeed hot, if not entirely clean. Mr. Dungaree washed his hands, rinsed his face, his stringy strands of hair. He disrobed and paper-toweled as much of the mud off his clothing that he could; and even restored the female slippers to their former pink shade of ugliness with some manhandling and ringing.

He stood in front of the electric hand dryer until he was reduced from drenched to decently damp.

Indeed, all hope was not lost.

When he passed by the *real* eggs on his way out, a teeny-bopper teen was scooping up the last of them, dumping them unceremoniously into the mouth of a carton, and Mr. Dungaree didn't even snarl, externally.

The looming gray clouds had stopped their voluminous uproar.

Now the air smelled salty and fresh, just like Ocean Air scented lab freshener.

Mr. Dungaree hobbled behind the gas station, found his little hidden trail behind the blue trash receptacles (oh, how hideous the waste of resources) and removed the secret branches that hid his makeshift wooden-pallet-constructed home-away-from-home. Otherwise known as: not a *home* at all.

And his life-saving, cobbled-together-with-junk, time machine.

If it worked.

Which it *would* because LabCorp Technician #34 was at the top of his old geezer's game, yes he still was.

Mr. Dungaree plunked down in the wobbly, three-wheeled, heart-attack tipping-backward desk chair, and pulled out the final copper wire.

He got to work.

It took precisely two hours. Or would have—if Mr. Dungaree had a watch.

The assortment of stolen tools eyed their new master with respect as he lovingly aligned them on the mechanics red towel, rolled them into a bundle, and gently packaged them into a plastic grocery sack.

Never go anywhere without your tools.

Unless you've accidentally zapped yourself naked back into the historical past.

The time machine—mostly constructed from a Taser gun, laptop motherboard, the guts of a microwave oven, and a can of genetically modified and experimentally fermented tuna fish as the battery pack (ingenious!), plus other uninvented-yet sciences and molecular odds and ends—fit snugly into a second plastic grocery sack.

Mr. Dungaree did not say goodbye to his home, nor look back when he left.

Well, he looked back for a *second,* but only because he heard a scary branch snap. But no one was there.

The quaint, coastal town of Trinidad hummed and hawed about its normal weekday under cloudy skies; locals walking needlessly, beachgoers and fishermen driving impatiently down the wet residential hill to the wooden dock. Poop-dispensing seagulls swooped the sky and singsongingly called out: there's a balding target over here.

Mr. Dungaree had long ago been dismissed as a transient; his time in the town impermanent.

Suitable.

These were the people of the past. The *ancestors* of the people who had led to his future. And honestly, they could suck it all.

Except the real eggs. They didn't deserve to suck *real* eggs.

Somehow, in the future apocalypse, all the chickens had been killed.

It was the oddest worldwide phenomena—culturally unspecific. The chicken itself seemed to have an inherent genetic vulnerability, a protracted constitution for extinction.

It was more shocking than the actual end of the world, which everyone clearly expected: the disappearance of the global chicken had been a foul crime.

And all of humanity was guilty.

Mr. Dungaree sighed a deep sigh.

His hungry exhale steamed the air, and then a ray of sun broke through the clouds and scattered rainbows on the glassy surface of the sea, stealing the rest of his breath away.

He stood empty and transfixed.

He should be more respectful of the beautiful topside of the historical world.

Being the first person from the future to ever see it again (without holograms)—gorgeous stormy seawater, bespeckled with white caps all marching like soldiers of war toward the black jagged peaks of a rocky shore.

But—The Chicken Time Machine Project.

Mr. Dungaree had been named the lead scientist by the UB12 Chancellor; a great honor, indeed.

And he could not shuck the weight of a mandated responsibility off his shoulders.

Not even to enjoy a godly view.

Mr. Dungaree continued his trek with the grocery sacks, the perfect homeless person's accoutrement; they swung with their own awkward weight and painfully banged his shins.

Toward Mama's Pig 'N Pancake restaurant, on the busy corner of the main street in town, with the chicken pen in the backyard; because Mr. Dungaree would not fail. He would bring chickens back to the future.

And himself, as well.

Now all he needed was to wait for the cloak of darkness.

Mr. Dungaree found the perfect big scratchy bush to hide behind, catty-corner to the parking lot of his target location. His knees cracked with arthritis as he groaned and sat on a curb. Two dollops of biting cold slowly soaked up into his sit bones from the damp perch.

The bush smelled just like rosemary. Oh indeed, it *was* a rosemary bush.

He looked up to the sky and prayed it would not torture him with rain.

But the clouds had already pulled apart like cotton candy, and the cold blue heavens softly faded into water-color; orange and red pastels.

Then the black shadows grew.

And the last patrons left. And Mama, who looked to be about Mr. Dungaree's age, finally came out from the backdoor under a sunflower porch light. Mr. Dungaree could see her from his angle above her fence. She wiped her knuckles against a food-stained apron, her curly shock of old-lady hair fringed yellow and crazily aglow with the porch light.

Glancing secretively left and then right, she reached into her apron and pulled out a half-smoked brown cigar —lit it with a quick red flame.

She cocked her hip like a gunslinger and rolled the large offense between her fingers.

Took four puffs and the smoke sailed high up into the blue-black night. She snubbed the butt, wrapped it carefully in a napkin, and back into her apron the evidence was stowed.

Then Mama gently clucked and cooed and lovingly rallied all the magnificent chickens home to roost, shutting their coop door. She disappeared back from whence she came. The restaurant's screen door closed on a hydraulic delay, then smacked the doorframe with the last word.

The nightly ritual had drawn to a close.

All was quiet.

Nighttime had commenced in the sleepy town of Trinidad, and a time-machinist and chicken thief was about to implement his plan.

Mr. Dungaree tried to stand up but his arthritic knees hollered treason and stayed put. He manually straightened each leg, gave them a cheap, worthless massage, and then grabbed an arm of the thick rosemary bush and pulled himself onto his feet.

Both bags in hand, he hurriedly flopped in his pink female slippers across the street to the restaurant's fence. Pulling his first tool out of the grocery sack, he manhandled the lock, slinking into the shadows of Mama's backyard.

Indeed, the composting smell of chicken manure in the run—it was a huge comfort, a reminder of the proximity of the prize. He inhaled deeply. The mocha and clove puff of cigar smoke lingered in the air.

Mr. Dungaree smiled.

The second tool from the grocery sack was a small, previously trashed, penlight. Just enough illumination to slink to the coop door without tripping, and flip the latch.

He'd been in the sacred chicken house before. He knew the layout.

The chickens were quiet on the roost. A hen cooed, worried. But they seemed to ignore him, which was good.

By the blinking malfunction of the tiny light, Mr. Dungaree managed to set up his time machine on the coop floor. If his calculations were correct, he'd tuck a hen under an arm, and then fire the Taser at his own chest, catapulting them all back to the underground lab in the future —where The Time Machine Chicken Project had been stalled.

(Indeed, since Mr. Dungaree had accidentally left his scientific team without notice.)

Originally, he'd only meant to locate a chicken in time,

and pull it into the future. But in a giant catastrophe, he'd sent himself back to the chicken.

If Mama had ever told anyone of the day she'd seen Mr. Dungaree streak butt-naked in broad daylight from her chicken coop—well, Mr. Dungaree would be even more red-faced then he had been that day.

Surely she hadn't properly seen his face. Perhaps her eyes had been waylaid by his other parts.

The final copper wires clicked into place. The roost felt heavy, expectant. Chicken shadows seemed to move around the wooden room even though the chickens weren't even moving.

Their eyes were just blinking.

He gripped the electric Taser in his hand like a gun.

Then the screen door to the restaurant banged the doorframe like a scream. Oh no! Someone was coming!

Mr. Dungaree lurched forward to snatch a hen. They all squawked like murder. His fingers clenched a chicken's foot and he desperately yanked her into his armpit. "So sorry girl," he said. Then a blinding flash struck his eyes, brighter than an oncoming speed train.

"What in the dickens are you—" Mama said.

But Mr. Dungaree had squeezed the Taser's trigger.

And accidentally zapped Mama into the future.

Oh dear. It had happened again. He'd goofed.

The hen clucked and everything got really silent in the dark. Mama's big police flashlight rolled a little toward the corner and stalled, creating a very bright circle on the wall.

In the very far distance a lonesome dog barked.

Mr. Dungaree swallowed a lump in his throat.

He hadn't even figured out what to do yet when Mama burst back into the chicken coop, stark naked, and white as a ghost. Her hair was much longer and styled differently.

"Oh wow, that's still just as unnerving," she confessed. "And go on, close your damn peepers. I've been through this twice."

Mr. Dungaree squeezed his eyes.

He started to open his mouth to explain—

"And shut your trap, too."

MAYBE THERE IS SOMETHING TO BE SAID OF NEGOTIATION while chewing. Less talking, more agreeing.

That night, Mr. Dungaree spent a lot of time in Mama's back room, in her most upright chair, beside the fireplace which crackled and popped with warmth. She fed him scrambled eggs and pancakes.

Oh, the gloriousness.

Mr. Dungaree melted like a stick of butter.

After time traveling herself, Mama had no problem believing Mr. Dungaree and everything he knew about The Chicken Time Machine Project.

"So you did this all for the love of eggs?"

He nodded happily.

"The future was so wrong without the chicken?"

He nodded again. "Terribly wrong." He mumbled with a mouthful of eggs. "Breakfast would never be the same."

Well, Mama might have been gone for six months in the future, but she'd been zapped back to her departure time in the past. She'd been through a lot *there*, though. It was clear a lot weighed on her mind.

"They're worried about a grandfather paradox," she said.

"I know." It was logical. If you change too much of the past, you can wink yourself right out of existence in the future.

"We're on standby here, except for morning egg delivery."

"Rightly so," he said. "Standby it is."

"Can you be satisfied with washing dishes to start?"

Mr. Dungaree nodded.

Being trapped in the past with chickens and a brilliant chef was a bright future indeed.

THE SEA GIRL'S SURVIVAL

THE FIRST TIME thirteen-year-old Abigale Oats heard the phantom whisper, the strange sloshing, wave-lapping *shhh* sound—she was biting her lip and trying not to cry at noon recess at Walter Luther Middle School.

Under the heat of New Mexico's desert-orange basketball sun, not a drop of liquid water anywhere for a mile except for the dirty, snake-winding Rio Grande; that *shhh* sound forced Abby to glance left and right.

Maybe the other kids had snuck up behind her again.

Like they had in the bathroom.

But only a sea of crispy brown grass surrounded Abby, and the lonely pockmarked baseball field like a crater on a desolate moon, and a pretty earless lizard that did push-ups in the powdery dirt whenever Abby looked at it.

You, too, can exercise.

Walter Luther didn't even *have* a stupid baseball team.

Only the beheaded, skeletal tumbleweeds ran the

diamond, with their berserkers gait and regardless of rules at all.

The air smelled of the yellow chamiso field beyond the broken chain-link fence; the wild bush that locals said was stinky as feet and caused seasonal allergies, and the tourists thought was the epitome of an exotic desert fragrance.

The air right now was definitely nasty like a bloated fish rotting in an athlete's shoe. Abby might be brand new to the Southwest, but she had a local person's nose.

The dead fingers of the breathless September breeze, which was too hot and tired to push anything of substance, brushed only the finest hairs on Abby's neck under her short, curly mop of sweaty hair.

If hair can sweat.

The other seventh-graders played on the concrete schoolyard—where the basketball hoops stood tall, just like rust-colored dinosaur bones with netted, slack-hung jaws—the kids all laughing and shouting, their voices pushing the distance toward Abby through a shimmery sky curtain of heat waves.

But no one looked at her on the forbidden metallic bleachers. No one waved. No one said: Hey friend, what are you doing sitting out there all alone; are you okay?

Abby hunched on the fry-pan hot aluminum—which hadn't seemed too hot until she plunked down on the metal, and then after the burn of surprise, the pain felt alright.

As if her physical pain and emotional pain were natural born enemies, and would have a boxing fistfight inside her body, and the physical pain would win in a knockout.

Be the champion of her torment.

And then her stupid emotional tears would suck back in defeat, and she'd have on her normal face again; the one that could talk and smile without her big lip quivering.

Mr. Rodriguez in fifth-period math always called on her; because the Hispanics chewed gum, and the Indians passed paper notes. And that one Asian boy stuttered.

But Abby just learned math.

The bottom side of her fleshy thighs were probably getting a horizontal bacon imprint, or turning into pinched-up skin corduroy, because she'd been stupid enough to wear shorts. Not that shorts were stupid, but it was because she'd forgotten to shave her legs.

Looking ever so hairy and unpopular; and like an Anglo person from Alaska, too.

Because Anglo was unpopular. (And Alaska was total outer space.)

Actually, she basically had two skin colors: College-paper white or boiled-lobster red. Plus freckles and shocked out ginger hair. Which she could have done well, if she'd been reinvented as a fat clown, and liked scaring children. And was a creepy man.

Abby pinched her eyes closed.

There was no way the *shhh* sound could be real. No cell phone speakers to trick her. Nobody whispering behind her.

And it wasn't her own heartbeat. Couldn't be. It just didn't have the rhythm of a heart.

It sounded like a real, wet, blue sea.

THE SECOND TIME ABBY HEARD THE WATERY *SHHH* SOUND, IT was dark in the guest bedroom where she was wrapped up deep in itchy wool blankets on the rickety metal bed.

So dark black, that the darkness became a moody creature that exhaled its smoky pinon breath over her face when the red glow flickered out down the hall in the kiva fireplace—where step-grandfather Mesta cooked posole and beans—and then she couldn't tell if her eyes were really open or closed tight.

She might be swallowed by dark, be inside the digestive stomach juices of dark.

Churning around and around.

But when her eyes got dry; that's when she knew they were open to the air.

And staring at nothing but blackened memory; the squat room that had only an empty wooden dresser, the mug of Bic pens, the beeswax candle, and her messy traveler's suitcase stuffed inside the small, barren closet which was filled with everything she could carry.

The class-action lawyers and the social workers had the rest of her family's stuff in storage somewhere back in Alaska. Because the case had gone bigwig; had gone hush-tones and important.

And Mesta kept the legal correspondences hidden, maybe in a clever, manila folder. Slid in a furniture crevasse somewhere. Abby had tried to look around his house—but just with her eyes, not with her fingers.

She was a teleported stranger here.

At the dinner table awkward Mesta always mumbled, let's not talk of it now.

If not now, then *when?*

Mesta's adobe stank of cinnamon mouthwash. The smell had built up in Abby's nose—and even when she closed the bathroom door across from her bedroom, the mouthwash still ghosted through the air to haunt her.

Mesta had a gingivitis bone infection thing.

He was like super old. And when he spit in the sink, it wasn't always the sink.

A kindly man for sure, his eyes were soft and brown, especially when he said he didn't know where Abby's grandmother had gone, except she'd gone tropical when he stayed desert.

Left him on an adventure a year ago, but they didn't divorce, because they loved each other and she still sent him monthly checks.

So those lawyers were on it, making business-suit lawyerly calls. Until they located biological Grandma, Abby was stuck with non-biological Mesta—which got really confusing overall because he didn't even—because all the rest of Abby's biological family was—

—No.

Because of stupid deluxe new minivans that can seat the whole family except her, because she had the flu, for the hockey game; and mountain cliffs, and faulty class-action brakes.

And four funerals.

Practically overnight, Abby was put on a crowded commercial flight, stuffed into a seat like a cow, and sent to temporarily stay here in the stupid cinnamon-mouthwash barn where Mesta booted her out in the morning to graze, and the school booted her home in the afternoon back to her stall.

Where she stared at the plastered walls in her room. And followed the cracks with her eyes.

And Mesta hardly spoke much English though he spoke it just fine.

She couldn't even have a TV out here. No cell phone. And she hated to read.

And the blue watery *shhh* sound came back in the pitch dark.

Whispered up through the lumpy chicken feather pillow, through the cotton mattress, the mud brick floor. Up through the solid dark earth a thousand miles beneath her, until all that hard earth sloshed into real salty water.

Rocked her gently in her bed, and she opened her eyes, and the sun flared in a coppery-white flash. Her lips tasted of brine.

And on her cheeks, she felt a sticky, sea-salt hairspray.

The dream was of a turquoise ocean, and a big orange floating raft. And how Abby lay there on the boat bottom, her legs rolling back and forth, in and out of consciousness; her face slowly turning lobster red.

WHY GO TO SCHOOL.

Why not wander *away* from the 7:15 am bus stop, where Abby stood alone at the crossroads between this dirt road and that other dirt road, with a heavy backpack of school books, most of which she had only opened accidentally.

She crunched on the side of the road for twenty minutes in her brown leather piano loafers, which were too small and her feet bulged out, and cars passed now and then and made her cough in dust.

She rolled her ankle once and had to sit down and rub it.

The dust stuck to her shaved and moisturized legs.

Irritated red bumps flushed her calves.

All around New Mexico it was brown. And flat, or hilly and shrubby, and rocky where poisonous rattlesnakes could lay.

And there weren't even any famous green cactus she could see.

It was like God had made every other world ecosystem with care, and then it was the end of the sixth day and he was running late, so he just threw the creation leftovers out here like recycling.

The blue-sky forehead of the morning frowned with concern and watched Abby through its cyclopean sun eye, as if it might call in some mythic herding dogs to nip her ankles, to get her back into the bus line.

But a line of one unpopular person is not much of a line.

The river Rio Grande: It was sandy ground, woody

debris, muddy olive water that flowed soft like someone had left on their backyard hose and then magnified the effect into a whole long river that cut the Southwest in half.

A canopy of Cottonwood trees, thick brown trunks and orange fiery leaves cast a bedazzled shade; and Abby plunked down on the embankment to listen to the wide water gurgle and flow.

She unzipped her backpack, and the zipper bit her thumb.

Pulled out a purple cube of sugary gum to smack. Oh, but first a mint chocolate square. The mint made her ears tingle, and a languid breeze fingered her hair.

She dropped her school books into the water, let them float away. One by one, they were like a row of ducklings without a mother.

Even the math book swept away. Bye-bye math.

When Abby crunched back along the dirt road to Mesta's adobe, her backpack was light as air. Her shoulders were boingy springs.

"How was school," Mesta mumbled at the bean and posole dinner.

"Okay."

THAT NIGHT IN THE BED, IN THE DARK, WAS THE THIRD TIME Abby heard the watery *shhh* sound, and it came on so loud, and so fast—it sucked her all the way out of New Mexico in a flash.

She opened her eyes to the coppery flare of sunlight blinding her eyes.

Her vision streaked into a whiteout: But she remembered the slippery bottom of the orange boat, and her legs rocking back and forth, and how the salty sea spray itched inside her nose.

Riding the bed of an endless ocean.

"Shhh," a French woman spoke into Abby's ear. "It's okay, honey. It's okay."

"What's okay?" Abby asked.

The cyclopean sun's eye had her transfixed in a blinding ray. And a sweet metal tinge of blood coated her lips. "Why do you keep saying that?"

"Jamais deux, sans trois. Never twice, without thrice. It's okay, we will prepare." The small, minty hands of the unseen woman massaged Abby's burned face with paste, and fresh water dripped over her lips until she swallowed. And when Abby woke up, she was back in bed in New Mexico in the early dawn.

With dried blood from where she had chewed her lip.

She didn't go to school again.

Big puffy clouds roamed the wide desert sky as Abby cut through the pinon trees and trudged in her piano loafers to the bank of the Rio Grande.

For a second she swore she saw a rattlesnake, but it was just a stick. Her heart pounded. She had to find a grassy place to sit down all alone.

And that's when the emotional boxer stood up in the boxing ring like the Comeback King; and waves of grief pummeled Abby in the gut and she sobbed and sobbed, snot hanging out her nose in two thin ropes.

"I can't do it alone, Mom," she cried. Over and over, until she curled up on her side. Sand stuck to the snot on her cheek, and she thought: It's not sandpaper, it's *skin*paper. And it was gross.

When she sat up again, Abby was lighter. Her chest felt like it did when she got off the Ferris wheel at the fair.

That was a good memory. The Alaska State fair every year. Wow, the deep-fried meat coma, the classic aging rockers on stage, the lumberjack show and the Peninsula Racing Pigs. Even the RV and boat storage display. Ha-ha, and the twins won the cabbage weigh-off.

So funny.

Abby nudged off her loafers and dipped her toes into the Rio Grande. It was lukewarm, like a forgotten bath.

It was nice and refreshing, though. She waded into a soft and shallow bottom, and the mud swirled up and buried her feet. She sat down. And the river saturated her shorts and her underwear and she felt so daring, like a rule breaker.

A daredevil.

The mud swallowed her legs.

When she walked home, her piano loafers squeaking, her pants rolled up to the knees; the social worker, the one with a mustache, sat with a clipboard on the dash of his forest green Subaru, with a cell phone pushed against his ear, and his eyes not quite the color of Alaskan ice.

In school again; at noon recess, on the same hot bleachers.

When the *shhh* came, Abby squinted up at the cyclopean eye in the sky and said, "Just take me."

"God won't take us, honey," the woman on the raft said.

"Why?"

The big orange boat bobbed up and down and the endless turquoise ocean had turned choppy gray. Clouds swirled overhead like a giant might slowly be wielding a metal whisk, preparing to pour in more sky ingredients, maybe some thunder to rumble.

Abby managed to pull herself up on her elbows, the firm raft's edge supporting her neck. The air smelled like electricity.

The French woman in a bedraggled business suit sat beside Abby, arms and legs loose like a ragdoll, one sleeve torn off like a punk-rocker, and a white bra strap overstretched and sagging on her shoulder. Her wet, flat hair looked ironed to her face. One eye was swollen shut like a dark walnut.

"Jamais deux, sans trois." The French woman studied the angering sky, a warm wind fingering her battered clothing, fluttering the edges of the fabric. "You are my good luck charm, Abigale Oats."

Abby felt bothered.

Something familiar was missing. She was wrapped in plastic, and couldn't feel. That's it—numb and thick as rubber. Abby's body all over was numb.

"Why am I dreaming of dying on a raft?"

"You're not dreaming, honey." The French woman's voice floated away.

"Then how come I don't stay here?"

The French woman pulled her face away from the sky, as if she had been magnetically transfixed. The gathering storm reflected and swirled in her wild eyes. "No one stays here." And she reached out with her little hands, and grabbed Abby's hand, and it felt like she would never let go.

The fabric above her sleeveless arm went *pat-a-pat-a-pat*.

ABBY YANKED THE COVERS OFF HER BED. THE CREATURE THAT was the darkness shrank back as Abby struck a match and lit the beeswax candle on the dresser. The flame danced in shadows on the wall.

"Where is real?" she whispered to the dark. "You? Are you real?"

The candle flared, and the darkness turned and ran with its tail between its legs. Abby's bare toes gripped the smooth brick tiles of the floor. Mesta's old man snore carried down the hall. She yanked a wool blanket off the bed and wrapped it around her shoulders Indian style.

Carried the candle in its ceramic holder in one hand, squeezed the blanket closed in the other hand, and shuffled quietly to the front door; then out onto the still sun-warm flagstone porch, the blue-black night with the stars sneezed out overhead, and glistening with fuzzy, twinkling light.

The air smelled of creosote and sage.

Abby set the candle down on the sundial planter box.

Was she dead, too? This could be, like—the process of the afterworld where you work things through?

And the thought of the hidden manila envelope with the lawyers' correspondence came to mind, and that it was time to use her fingers to find it. So she slunk around the adobe house with her candle, trying not to light herself on fire, or wake up the sleeping snorer. And *nowhere* was the manila that she could find.

It was only an afterthought: The neglected mailbox.

So back out into the blue-black, star-sneezed night, in her piano loafers and crunching over the gravel driveway to the rusty metal mailbox propped up on a stick.

It squeaked open.

There lay a crisp white letter.

Ten minutes later, cross-legged on her bed with the candle flickering on the dresser: Abby knew her grandmother had been found by the high-tech lawyers. And she held the one-way ticket to Honolulu in her shaking hands. Business first class.

The flight left in one day.

Abby's heart pounded in her ears.

Jamais deux, sans trois. So the plane would crash over the water. Impossible! The second tragedy in her life, and bad things came in threes. But not if she could warn them—warn everyone.

When dawn broke the night, and the snoring stopped and the toilet flushed, and Mesta had his steaming cuppa joe at the kitchen table—Abby slunk out of the guest room and pulled out a wooden chair to sit across from him.

The chair's legs were uneven. It tilted back and forth with a soft *clonk* on the tiles until she sat rigidly upright.

Sausage sizzled crazily in a pan.

"I'm suposta go to Hawaii tomorrow but we have to reschedule it." Abby pushed the letter across the table, but she kept the ticket inside the envelope, clasped in her hand.

Mesta took a century to read the letter with his reading glasses perched low on his nose. He got up and flipped the pigs in the pan, then shuffled to Abby and handed her the letter back personally, then sat down in his spot.

"Why don't you have a phone," she said.

He took a long coffee sip, and looked at Abby with kindly brown eyes. "I'm peculiar." That was his explanation.

Abby leaned forward and the broken chair gave a loud *clonk*. She put her hand over her mouth so she wouldn't shout, because she suddenly felt like shouting.

"They want you in the school," he said. "But why listen to them? Your last day in the *desierto,* and a fine one it should be."

Abby thought that maybe a hundred random people were going to die tomorrow. Crashed at sea. And a fine day this last one would not be.

She rushed to school.

She asked to see the principal, but he was out today. She found Mr. Rodriguez in the hallway, and showed him the letter, and tried to say that the plane might crash, but

Mr. Rodriquez just said, I will miss you in class, you bright young lady.

She talked the front desk secretary into handing her the push button phone. But when the airplane operator came on, and said how may I help you—Abby hung up instead.

At recess she sat on the hot aluminum bleachers only long enough to scan the playground, to make sure no one was looking, and then she escaped through the broken chain-link fence into the yellow chamiso field.

She didn't even think of the stinky feet smell. She just clutched the envelope to her chest.

The bushes tickled her sensitive legs.

The front seam on her left piano loafer broke open, and her toe squeezed out and pinched on a rock.

"Maybe it's not a second chance with Grandmother," she whispered. She looked up into the cyclopean portal in the sky; into the whiteout, into the doorway in her mind.

RAIN HOWLED AND ROARED IN A SLATE GRAY TEMPEST, OCEAN spray kicked Abby's face with needles. The French woman got dunked, her wet hair became an iron helmet over her face; in the metallic flash of lightening, a medieval knight-in-armor.

Screaming inside a faceless shell.

Up and down the raft bucked.

Abby's legs swishing far left, then far right.

And she couldn't hold onto the life rope.

Anymore.

ABBY LAY DOWN IN THE CHAMISO FIELD, ON HER BACK, UNDER a canopy of thirsty flowers. The hard dirt. The feeling of being invisible, and not having to do anything.

If I die there, will I vanish here?

But she thought long and hard about it again—about being in two real places, and the doorway opening and closing. And she decided that one place had to be unreal.

Had to be a sideways place. Another land. A mental landscape.

But which one?

Oh Jesus, but what if a rattlesnake comes by. Abby rolled up on her elbows and then rolled over to her knees and then stood up all covered with dust.

Suddenly, the field was creepy, with too many rocky places for poisonous things to hide. She didn't want to be in the creepy field.

She didn't want to be in New Mexico, even.

She wanted to be in Alaska, before the—

Before everything went to shit.

And it seemed suddenly that Abby had never directly asked for what she needed. Had never thought she could. Had never dared dream it possible. But *now* she dared.

Because it was almost too late.

She was letting go of the rope in the real world.

"Mommy, come help me," she cried. "Come here and help me. I need you. I can't live without you."

A figure materialized, standing in the golden field, the

sun a perfect halo around her familiar shape, the golden light pouring out from behind her.

And Abby ran to her mother's outstretched arms, and she cried until the sorrow turned to wonderment, and then to joy—and then into the gift of *knowing.*

The sky rotated to night, because they needed to walk among the mysteries of the stars: Because the stars hold the secrets of all things.

And all souls journey.

Destiny awaits you, my sweet child, and though I can no longer be with you physically on Earth—my love, you will never be alone—I will always be quietly by your side. May this give you courage.

Right now, you are fighting between life and death, and your mind has been drifting between the physical world and a dream-story you've made up because you're injured and anguished. If you keep telling yourself a story you will give up and die.

It is not time to die. You must be brave. There are future souls who await your touch. There are promises you have made, lives you must intersect, people only you can help.

Will you abandon them now? The choice is yours. For as you choose it; it will be.

THE TEMPEST SEA HAD TURNED INTO A LONELY, CALM, BLUE bath.

The life raft had mostly deflated.

One compartment of air inside the orange rubber still gallantly buoyed. Abby and the French woman clung to it, the white safety rope. Had their hands and arms wrapped around it.

And all together they were a giant's wrung-out bath toy—abandoned, left to sink down into an oceanic drain.

"I'm a curse," Abby said.

"No, no—not that," the French woman laughed. "You *survived* three times. You *survived.*"

And the positive side of the meaning sank in, and Abby laughed, because she felt like a wine cork, bobbing up and down as they drifted. "You're my new lawyer from across the isle on the plane. And you apologized about the firm, and me being sent to Mesta. And you were explaining my case before the plane crash."

"Hi, I'm Claudine."

"I'm Abigale."

And they both laughed so much with the wild absurdity that they almost drown, but they held each other up above the bath of warm, turquoise water; and laughed more and more.

After awhile they were quiet again.

Claudine glanced at her watch, which had stopped telling time. "We missed the meeting at Santon and Fischer."

"That line out there, see the shimmer rising up. See the brown?" Abby asked.

"I think that's the big island we're floating to. We were not that far out from Hawaii when the plane crash happened."

Wow, it was an island sanctuary in the middle of all the nothingness. And Abby felt like she needed to remember something important, something like a dream—but floating with her chin barely above the sea, nothing else came to mind, just the reality of the crash.

And her overpowering will to live. No matter what.

Then, they heard the Coast Guard rescue helicopter blades chopping the sky, and bright orange-clad rescue people signaling frantically with their hands from the open helicopter doors, strong ropes descending.

Abby reached up.

THE ORDINARY

TOMAS STOOD under the capstone of an ornate stone archway painted with the mysterious language of the priests. He trudged out onto the cold stone slab of the mezzanine, the high mountain mists blue-gray and swirling as if stirred by a giant's breath.

The breeze carried up the fragrance of the tamarind orchards in the summertime valley below, sun-sweetened and wild, but there was something else that Tomas noticed in the early dawn—his own fermented reek of fear.

It rose off the bruised rash on his neck, his sweaty armpits.

He adjusted his beloved zafu cushion tucked in his arm.

The mezzanine launched out into the high altitude mists like a suicide platform, a half-circle dangling in space. It was bordered only by a one-foot high stone wall that any fool could trip off and fall to his death.

Of course, the whole stone monastery had been carved out of the face of the mountain by long-ago ancestors that no one remembered anymore.

Maybe they had all fallen off?

In the early morning, the smooth stone floor of the mezzanine was cold and littered with crystalline dewdrops that glimmered like liquid stars, the sun just now rising over the highest peaks of the Senoche range to the east, a coppery hue burning through the clouds like a medallion in the sky.

Out here, Tomas's balance betrayed him, he sometimes felt his body tilting down in a sickening slide toward the edge.

But he had never slid, not really. It was an illusion.

The monastery was full of little tricks and mind games, spirits flitting through the stone walls with devilish thoughts and projections.

But on this morning the structure in the sky echoed with its own stony silence.

The monks slept. The teenage boys slept.

Tomas did not sleep.

His bare toes wiped through the dewdrops and he left a trail of shy, flat footsteps leading to the meditation slab, a raised flat seat in the center of the mezzanine surrounded by a clay pot holding a clean cloth, an incense box and snuffer, and the *honsha* ball.

This stupid ball was a ten pound, circular weight made of antique apple-red and bronze ore.

Tomas swept the dew off the flat seat with the clean

cloth and carefully lay his zafu cushion down. He sat in prayer position, legs folded, his brown linen pants and shirt comfortably folding around his too-thin frame.

A bead of sweat cut a slow line down his brow, then swooshed under the bridge of his nose into his left eye. It stung. He blinked and now it was a tear that escaped and fled down his cheek.

No one would know.

He wouldn't let them know.

Tomas thought of his parents far below in the central village.

Would the morning sun warm the cooking hearth as Mother boiled quail eggs and mixed a paste of amaranth and water for the morning *canche?* Would his parents later walk the fields together, working shoulder to shoulder, brown hands glistening with the fertile heat of the afternoon sun? Talking little because they already knew everything that shouldn't be said? Would the dark night come to find them huddled in their buckwheat bunk, arm in arm, still whispering goodnight to their son in their softest joined voice—the son missing for seven years but still everyday his safe return the first and last prayer on their lips?

In Tomas's fantasies, these were the images of his parents he conjured.

But in truth, it was hard to remember them well anymore. It was hard to recall the exact rise of their cheekbones, or the curve of their eyes. The exact tone of their skin—cinnamon like his, or clove like many of the other boys? He didn't want his memory to fade away. To leave him abandoned, a hollow product of the kidnapping, a seventeen-year-old who had lost his origins. Without a beginning to hold on to.

Just an end to fear.

Tomas inhaled and his ribs felt tight enough to splinter his lungs.

He closed his eyes, beginning the meditation, working through the breathing structures, dropping down into the mind state of *bocane,* and then *sandhi.* Softly, his worries faded, his muscles relaxed. The splintered feeling in his ribs released.

Meditation practice offered the only escape.

That was the lure. It was what the monks demanded of the boys, but it also afforded a refuge from reality. Tomas caught all his worries in a mental sieve and they busied themselves with draining away—far away.

Eyes still closed, quieter and quieter, he now rose into the universal stillness, beyond space and time, into the lightness of being.

His thoughts echoed somewhere in the vastness below as his consciousness floated in bliss. Unconditional love wrapped its arms around him and nurtured his soul.

Yet today, a single worry nudged him, shook him.

No more time. There is no more time.

That warning zinged with alarm up his spine. So Tomas left the place of healing love and consciously lifted his dirty hands to his slender face, fingers upright and clenched tight. His own fermented stink escaped his armpits, and yet the smell was distant, as if from another world.

He opened his eyes wide.

He saw nothing but the ordinary darkness of his palms covering his face.

Failure again, over and over and over.

He was supposed to be able to waken his spiritman, to see *through* his own hands and to vision. He was supposed to levitate the *honsha* ball like the other boys, and train and master the dark arts.

Of all the chosen boys, only Tomas had no gift. Only Tomas was a mistake.

He peeked through the cracks in his fingers.

The black monk sat on the edge of the mezzanine. His frightful eyes were tiny specks of light under the deep-set hood of his black cloak, framed only by the suggestion of human cheeks.

"This is the day of your final test." The black monk spoke with his smoky, cavernous voice. "Are you a useless one, Tomas? Do you have no gift?"

Tomas's ribs squished his breath out. Anxiety coiled around his neck, the rash flushing. He couldn't be useless.

The mists had turned golden flanged, still swirling in the movement of a phantom giant, but now revealing sky and the white peaks of the mountain range to the east. To the south, the faint emerald hue of the tree line fell into the river-cut valley below and the central village where Tomas had once known laughter and love.

The boys did not laugh at the monastery.

"You will manifest, or I will send the order for your parents' death tonight. Maybe your own."

Tomas wasn't sure if he heard the powerful monk's voice from inside or outside his own mind.

"I know," Tomas whispered.

"What is that?"

"I will do it," Tomas repeated louder, but his voice cracked. He felt his spine fold, as if he were trying to curl his entire body under the cover of skin-and-bone hands.

A hideous sound, a soft clattering like leaves and rattlesnake tails, rose from the swish of the monk's robes when he stood.

Tomas peered again through the cracks in his fingers over his face.

The black monk pointed at the *honsha* ball with a long index finger and the ore levitated off the rack, floating like a bobber on an invisible fishing line. *Bang,* the heavy ore slammed back into its holder.

The monk needed say no more. He left, a broken trail of dewdrops in his wake.

Tomas shook on his zafu, weeping the stinging tears, and no longer cared who knew.

THE WHOLE DAY PASSED, AT ONCE BEAUTIFUL AND TERRIBLE.

Tomas did not eat or drink. He obediently practiced meditation and tried to levitate the stupid ball, stretching his legs every hour.

Refusing to give up because all the other boys stolen from the village had levitated the *honsha* and saved their own parents.

He felt the boys' eyes, at different times during the day —staring at his back and watching him from hidden places in the monastery.

Snickers echoed between walls.

When dusk arrived, a cut of magenta bled the sky all the way into the horizon, the distant haze of the fabled desert of the Nobu tribes out there somewhere.

He remembered it was where his mother's people lived.

Rattlesnake rattles struck with each footfall as the black monk approached from behind, swept past Tomas, and stood in his customary place near the mezzanine edge, his back turned.

"You fail us," the monk said. "You have not opened your third eye."

The pressure clogged in Tomas's throat. The fever-red, bruised handprint around his neck cinched his esophagus closed.

The monk whirled around, his shiny eyes sharp pinpoints of light inside his deep hood.

Tomas couldn't draw a breath so he stumbled to his feet, his neck muscles beaded like thin ropes. The mezzanine started to slant, to pitch forward.

"Please don't kill my parents," Tomas begged. "My parents love me, I know they do." He stumbled forward a few steps.

The monk's eyes flashed with annoyance.

"I can lift the *honsha,"* Tomas shouted.

"No you can not," the monk fired back. "You are useless!"

Tomas burned in shame, the rash spreading down into his chest, squeezing his heart with a fist. Tomas reached out and grabbed the stupid circular orb. For five years he had never imagined touching it physically because that was forbidden, never imagined doing anything but exactly what he was told. The black monk's sorcery terrified him. Everyone.

Suddenly Tomas realized the heavy *honsha* was light as a feather. In fact, it was hollow inside.

Now the stupid ball seemed even more stupid than ever.

"Who cares about waking the spiritman and manifesting powers," Tomas shouted. "You're just a mean person who controls the village and kidnaps children."

Tomas threw the ball, his arm unwound like a slingshot.

The sacred *honsha* was finally airborne under Tomas's command, arching up toward the monk and his black hood, white pinprick eyes, and the deep-set suggestion of a human face.

The monk's arm casually reached up to catch the ball. He stepped backward. His foot bumped the edge of the mezzanine wall. He lost his balance. In a sickening moment he pitched over the edge, robes billowing up then flapping down and all at once utterly gone.

Tomas couldn't believe it. Did his torturer just—die? Tomas gulped the thin mountain air. The platform pitched hard on Tomas, he felt dizzy, stumbled forward. He crawled on his knees across the stone and looked over the edge.

The gathering mist in the air dropped away like a vacuum at the end of the world, swirling down in the twilight toward rocky spires and sheer descents.

See, it *wasn't* totally unreasonable that the ancients had all fallen off the edges of the monastery long ago.

Tomas backed away on all fours, dragging the seat of his pants. He noticed his mouth hung open. He snapped it shut.

When the dizziness ended, he stood.

Someone shuffled behind him and Tomas turned to see all the subordinate monks in brown robes and all the teenage boys in brown linen staring speechless at him, gathered underneath the ornate stone archway.

No one moved. They *all* had feared the black monk. And now that fear was homeless, upset.

Tomas picked up his zafu and cradled it under his arm.

The monks and the teenage boys parted for Tomas to pass under the capstone. Tomas could feel the electricity of their eyes on his skin—and no one snickered now.

Tomas knew they all had super powers. He had witnessed all kinds of strange and frightening manipulations of objects and fire and illusion and time. They could have stopped his escape, but they didn't. They could have even killed him, but they didn't.

It was a culture of dueling to the death. In the eyes of the necromancers, Tomas had dueled the black monk and won.

"Come home with me?" Tomas suggested.

The other teenage boys and the subordinate monks didn't move. Shock had rooted them to the stone floor.

He felt like he should say more to them, but he didn't know what to say. When Tomas walked out of sight, no one followed.

Tomas hurried down the dangerous steps, the *only* path down from the mountaintop—cliffs dropping into a wide, toothless abyss right beside him, his one arm still cradling the zafu, the other clutching rocky holds and crevasses. His own stink soured his nose.

The magenta sky faded to blue-black.

His foot slipped with a sickening *swoosh.*

Tomas slammed onto his butt, one leg shooting off the path into space, his right hand clutching a jagged edge.

A cascade of baby rocks waterfalled into nothing and the zafu flew away.

A strange gurgle escaped his throat as he dangled. The black monk's body lay crumpled on a ledge, the white skin of his half-smashed face illuminated by the prodding fingers of moonlight, bloated fisheyes crooked and helpless and blank staring. A pool of blood shined like black oil.

Tomas wiggled up and away, his weak arms fired with adrenaline.

He tucked into a hollow and sat with his spine against the mountain and his knees held tight to his chest. He shivered a little, tucking his filthy linen shirt into his pants for warmth. He studied the path leading back up to the towering monastery, already shrunken in size with distance.

Still no one followed.

The midnight view was extraordinary. The moon floated in the sea of sky. The cliff faces rose left and right around him, the rocky legs of the slumbering giants, the path he wanted to follow barely visible, a faint glow in the moonlight, a silver ribbon of steps leading down and down and down to the valley.

It would take most the night, but he would be in his parents' arms come morning. They could escape to his mother's homelands in the desert, too far for sorcery to find them.

But maybe Tomas didn't want to return to his village only to lose it again. Maybe there was a way life could be like his beautiful meditations. Like the childhood he wanted to remember.

His old zafu was gone anyway. There had to be a new hope.

And then he knew.

Tomas, the weak boy who could not manifest a gift, had all along the greatest power of all—the place of unconditional love in his meditations. No one else at the monastery had found this source. That's what they were missing. That's why they couldn't leave.

They knew only fear.

Tomas stood up slowly, his body stiff and joints swollen. There was something he had to do.

In the dark light of the moon, Tomas inched down to

the ledge where the dead monk lay and took the robe from his body. The reign of sorcery had ended.

He began the climb back up the narrow mountain steps, the robe over his shoulder. It was just for effect. Tomas couldn't leave until they all followed. Until they all left together. He knew he wasn't useless.

He knew his gift was the greatest.

THE HUTSU HUNTER

A GLOSSY RED handprint dripped in blood from the wrought iron handle, so I used my shoulder to shove a clean area of the solid oak door to the entrance of the Three Seasons Tavern.

The heavy slab of wood stuttered open on broken hinges, as if the door was experiencing its own personal earthquake. Then it bucked in the sudden throes of death, rocked off its rectangular frame, and slammed cockeyed onto the stone floor with a boom.

So much for a graceful entrance on my part.

But then, I'm an old woman, and grace took her leave of me long ago. I'm a knot of strong, spindly legs, purple keloid scars crisscrossing my desert-brown skin—which is stretched and cracked over my roughened knuckles—and the long, white, braided hair of a hutsu hunter.

Though not every witch hunter has white hair, or a long braid, or is even human.

But we are all old. And we are all professional hunters, if you want to call us professional. We hunt practitioners of the darkest arts, we hunt real evil.

Man, woman, or otherworldly—the worst of their kind.

My oldest scar is an ivory quarter moon under my right eye, a bloodless memory sliced long ago into my face. My eyes are still the midnight-blue of my birth, a watery hue.

Two lovers once told me a story about my eyes: they were dark, guarded oceans that almost never revealed my true weaknesses. That I was hiding down in there, under stormy waves. They said that loving me was like floating in a tiny boat over drowning seas. You can look down, but you don't want to fall in.

Those two people were murdered. I don't think about them anymore. I can't think about them, or I won't want to go on living and do the job I need to do.

I keep to the shadows. When I squint, my eyes can appear almost black.

I use this to my advantage.

No one trusts an old woman with black eyes.

When I loosen my spine and focus my Qi, I still move lightly on the balls of my feet. Light as a feather like the best of the young kickfighters. But when I'm weary from days of hard travel, the limp sneaks back into my right hip and shortens my gait, just like an old friend who won't go away.

Because I don't want any friends.

Well, *they* would stubbornly argue that fact, but I'm allowed my own opinion.

Though I guess I'm not being fair to the three riffraff hutsu who care about me. Shote, a human desert crawler like me, born and baked under the hot suns; Dahl, the merman who prefers land and a breathing apparatus because being one-quarter fish wasn't enough for the Acasci Sea; and Komb, one of the very last giant dwarfs from the Island of Vale.

For the record, because it amuses me: a giant dwarf is basically the size of an exaggerated human, but the brawn and moodiness and wooly mammoth body hair is larger than life.

I tell my traveling comrades all the time they shouldn't care about me. We lose the things we care about in this blackened, perilous world.

Of course we do.

I'd rather not burden them with another loss. We've all had *that* kind of loss, those of us who scour the land in search of horror. We put ourselves in harm's way, and we get harmed.

All I get from my three friends when I push them away are hearty scoffs. Well, actually, the verbal scoff comes from the giant dwarf—he's the only one who can grumble like an earthquake in a lovingish way.

Over the last few days I've caught him watching me out of the narrowest corner of his amber eye, the only one he has left. Even his overgrown hedge of eyebrows couldn't conceal the concern in his ricochet glances—when he pretended to be looking elsewhere, but was really reading me.

I knew he *knew.*

Well, he was right. I *was* planning to go vigilante. I was planning to leave our little traveling group. What he didn't know was that it would be so soon.

That it would be last night.

I slipped my three companions a secret dose of sweetbark as we all sat around the campfire drinking bitter oxbeer, laughing in good humor, mesmerized by the blood-orange coals flickering as we cooked a bladder of muskweed stew under a charcoal sky.

When my companions slipped helplessly into a paralytic sleep, I chained up Komb's stubborn sandcat, named Garange, who hissed savagely at me with her jade eyes. Her chameleon fur went from its natural translucent shimmer to the deep red of smoldering embers, and she flattened her ears and bared her ivory fangs. Saliva even dripped off of them. I'd have to say that cat was mad. She's enormous—her boulderish head is level with my chest—but she's felt the crack of my whip and doesn't dare bite me again.

I have enough scars, we don't need to be adding to them.

I chased off my comrades' horses—and now here I am, a hard night and a harder day's ride away in the Whistler Valley, in a migratory agricultural village called Machu, near the Elopian Mountains.

Alone.

Because some of the things we hutsu hunt, we must hunt alone.

A frightening supernatural witchcraft, called *makukun,* has gained power across these lands over the centuries. A black magic that can perform unusual horrors, such as reanimating the corpses of children and—well, it's all gruesome stuff.

I know because I was forced to train as a *makukun* practitioner with other children long ago.

Now—I'm reconditioned.

(That's a story for another time.)

The legends go that the hutsu are old souls called to save the future, and they speak in the language of the ancients, The Invisible Ones, from whom they draw some of their traditions. The hutsu are esoteric wise folk who have lived many lives on Gwyndor, and are given extreme hardship in life to prove an allegiance to serve the Light.

Now to be honest, the last thing I'd call myself is wise. No wise woman ever feels wise enough. And to be even more honest, I took quite the circuitous path toward goodness.

Just like any good hutsu.

But the less the villagers know about their mysterious healers, the centenarians of the Northern Peaks, the better. We wouldn't want to scare anyone.

Though we are true medicine healers, as varied in shape and size and race and temperament as the wind blows, and true enough—we heal with our hands.

But the same hand that giveth, also taketh away.

So don't ask me to save your life, I may not be in the giveth frame of mind.

And now, with the bloody tavern door laying broken on the floor behind me, I wasn't sure I could even see my own hands right in front of my face. The abandoned building was as pitch black as the starless night behind me. The apple fragrance of the nearby orchard carried in with the cold night air and battled the warm, coppery rise of fresh blood.

My stomach clenched.

The tavern was eerily quiet, too.

I stumbled forward blindly and met a solid wall with the tough end of my leather travelers boot. A hollow thud reverberated and gritty dust sprinkled my forehead, tasting acrid and making me sneeze.

I tried to spit but my dry mouth was spitless.

I reached to the waist of my leather pants and unlatched my twelve-foot bullwhip. It trailed straight behind me, perpendicular to my hips. The familiar grip fits perfectly in my palm, the smooth leather worn to the curve of my fingers. I've done target work all my life. I can cut, strike, or tie my target in a split second, and I've got a cracker on the end of the fall that sounds like the devil himself.

Or herself, as the case may be.

I stood still as granite, swallowed up in shadow. Closed my eyes so I could sharpen my sixth sense.

I sensed nothing.

But I knew *she* was here. Had to be the one here. I'd risked everything for *her* to be physically *here.*

The visions had started a year ago. I'd be in a room with my traveling comrades and suddenly she'd be standing alone in a corner watching me, like a ghost, but not a ghost. No one else could see her. Hatred trembled in her midnight-blue eyes. Trembled and trembled.

We were both spellbound.

After all these years.

I don't know what she saw in my eyes, but I bet it was fear.

I'm not above fear.

Time passed and the visions increased. I learned to focus my meditations, to find her somewhere far across Gwyndor in a foreign land, I knew not where. I studied the wrinkles around her eyes, the way the darkness pooled in impenetrable layers, and I thought of our childhood. And I thought of injustice.

We were magnetically fascinated with each other. Addicted to this morbid new cat-and-mouse game. What would it have been like to be the other if the tables had been turned? If she had been rescued, and not I?

My fascination became my obsession, my dirty little secret.

Because I didn't tell my traveling comrades of my visions, and sometimes an omission becomes a lie. Not always. But sometimes.

The secret visions got stronger. *She* was first to manifest the ability to speak into our mind. We cut each other with words. Threatened and teased: but threatened more. The only thing we never did was laugh, not really. All the smiles were jousts.

I felt as though she hated me.

I didn't want it to be true.

That we would one day physically meet alone was clear. Destine, because we wanted that destiny. Thinking back on it now, I don't know why I made that decision. I felt guilty, that was why.

When we'd realized our individual travels had led us from distant lands into the same valley, led us into a physical proximity that was too utterly tempting to refuse, we'd agreed on this tavern as a meeting location.

Tonight.

But this bloody handprint on the tavern door—I hadn't known what she would do. I promise I hadn't known or I wouldn't have allowed it to happen.

It was too late now.

I took a few blind steps, the wet mud on my traveler's boots sloughing off with my first footfalls into the establishment, creating a soup-slurping noise against the stone floor.

Oddly appropriate, considering I'd noticed the sign outside for seasonal apple-and-lamb stew.

I turned a corner and continued down what must have been a hallway—sensing my way in the dark, my fingers interpreting the surfaces of splintered wood, cold, cracked stone, and goopy wet substances that I wiped off on my leather pants.

I tripped over a tumbled chair, climbed through a maze of objects; moving deeper into a building that only a few hours before had been a brightly torchlit roadhouse full of hungry folks.

To my left, a weak yellow glow spilled against a wooden wall like the early light of dawn from an unseen window, and then, around a final corner, a mighty fire roared in an enormous stone hearth, orange-and-purple flames writhing like snakes in the logs.

Though the perimeter of the cavernous room lurked in shadow, an army of giants could have served their ranks supper and still had room to dance the jig.

Now the establishment lay in smoky ruins.

I coughed as the smoke burnt my throat.

I guess I was late to the party.

There wasn't much time before a posse of local horse riders, alerted by the survivors of this chaotic scene, would encircle the Three Seasons Tavern to deal with this bizarre situation in their own, not exactly wizened, way.

Swords and battle-axes and rope darts would be drawn, and those weapons would be useless against the supernatural. More people would die tonight.

I needed to be done and long gone by then.

The ghostly purplish firelight flickered over splintered wooden tables, high-backed chairs, and hand-carved benches, all tossed hither-thither and snapped like matchsticks in a hurricane. The fire popped and crackled, the oxygen-sucking hiss of an engorged blaze greedily smacking its lips for more food.

What was burning so hungry in that hearth besides the wood?

I could almost hear the haunted echoes of the evening's patrons as their joyful, hearty laughter had mingled with the clank of metal spoons and the harmony of the musical bards playing their windy instruments.

All of that hubbub would have slowly turned into shocked silence in the moments just after the psychic destruction began—until the first screams caused a cascade of panic and everyone ran.

Well, the smart ones ran, because those who stayed to fight would be dead bodies under my feet.

Far across the room, a lone female stood before the flames, unsteady on her feet, an orange-colored flange outlining her silhouetted skin like an eclipse of the sun. Her head tilted oddly to the side.

Her back was turned to me.

A naked woman, from the curve of her hips. A new woman.

She'd hadn't seen twenty winters yet.

I felt a strange squeeze in my chest, as if an unidentified emotion was building there, wanting to get out. An uncomfortable disgust.

The firelight sparkled through gaps in her long hair in ripples of molten copper. Her bare arms hung at her sides, firelight streaming through thin, sickly, long fingers.

I wasn't sure what she was, exactly.

In witchcraft, things can be deceiving.

Every hair on my neck stood up and flushed me with warning. My fingers had a death grip on my whip handle. A normal person would run for their life. I can run like the wind, but it's too late to save my life.

I'll save myself in the next world, I hope.

I'll finally have gotten things set right by then.

I stepped forward, darkness blanketing the floor like a black void. My boot sank into something mushy, which almost held my weight, but popped like a bladder. A wash of unseen liquid gurgled out in the shadows, and the updraft of bile saturated the air around me. Okay, not a bladder. A full stomach.

Nausea punched my guts.

A salty line of sweat beaded across my upper lip, the moisture slipping between my lips. I sucked at it.

Salt is a good flavor. I focused on the taste of salt.

There is only salt.

"This is wrong, Kata." I shouted into the room so my words might carry. "These people were innocent." My usual strong voice came out weak in the cavernous black space, as if the blackness had eaten it.

I stepped forward again, kicking my boot out so that some of the tissue slung off and splattered somewhere. I heard it smack.

The hungry fire continued to flick too high up the edges of the hearth, a thousand ravenous serpent tongues licking the flat stone masonry, trying to reach up to the thatched roof.

The unfamiliar silhouetted figure bent down like a jerking puppet, folding awkwardly in half in the dark and disappearing for a moment, then standing exaggeratedly upright. Off-balance. Her long fingers flicked something liquid into the hearth that made the flames roar and hiss.

Some kind of accelerant. Maybe *bakcumoth*. Or another flesh ferment.

The coppery skin of her back glowed in a sweaty sheen in the reinforced heat. Her spine curved, vertebral ridges undulating. Long black hair fell past her shoulders, the tips curling up, frizzing a little.

Or maybe even singeing.

The smoke smelled bitter and rank. Not just rank—it smelled revolting.

I was halfway across the dark room by now and I could see a little better in the growing purplish light.

A fractured table blocked my path, one wooden leg sticking straight up from a round belly like a dead pig in rigor mortis. I sidestepped it.

Just a little closer than twelve feet now, because I measure the world around me by the length of my whip's strike.

The naked figure turned to face me. Beads of sweat dripped off her taut breasts, down her stomach, where heat rashes pooled in growing rings. Her eyes were swollen, vacant. Mismatched pupils, so that she looked as if her head had been shaken and her eyes dislodged.

One arm hung cockeyed, disjointed. A white gleam of fresh bone poked out of the skin at the elbow.

In her fingertips she held a man's severed head, clutched by his curly black hair, his eyes bulging out like sheeny obsidian stones.

The reanimated corpse of a girl—holding the dead head of a man.

Fortunately, there was more salt drenching my upper lip.

Salt.

Salt.

There is only the smell and taste of salt.

The girl corpse turned her back to me again, lobbed the heavy head with both hands, its hair streaking, mouth agape, yellowish teeth barred in death like a strange donkey. The forehead thudded into the top of the stone hearth with a sickening smack, like an overripe pumpkin, but the head still fell into the flames anyway.

The face boiled and melted off its bones.

I got chills. Worse than chills. Fingers slid in between my ribs with an icy squeeze and pressed out all my breath.

Evil really goes all out for the hideous, extravagant performance. Now that I am on the side of Light, I can tell you we keep things simple over here.

"Won't get what you want." A strange voice gurgled out of the corpse's crushed throat, her jaw flapping, chewing her own tongue like a pink piece of meat. "You shouldn't have come here, Wynd."

I'd had enough.

I flicked my wrist.

My bullwhip cracked out like black lightening and cinched around the poor dead thing's ankles, yanking her feet from under her, slapping her to the ground. The corpse didn't get up again.

Sometimes you have have to disrupt the evil performance, part the curtains, and get backstage.

"Enough, Kata," I said. "Come out."

"Haven't I given you what you wanted?" A familiar voice spoke from behind me. We had the same voice. Except Kata's was deeper, smokier. "A little show-and-tell?"

I had the distinct feeling something supernatural had gathered behind me in the dark, something hulking and huge.

I felt the first pinprick on my exposed neck, the sharp edge of a single splinter. Then another.

Then another.

I slowly cranked my head to look over my shoulder.

A swarm of splinters hovered in the air, tiny tips reflecting in the firelight, a million angry spikes of wood ready to pierce my eyes, porcupine my face, wiggle and swim and stab every cell in my body.

"Really?" I said. "You're so insecure you have to act like a show-off?" If I'm not above fear, I'm not above bluffing bravado, either.

The splinters dropped to the ground with a delicate, tinkling sound. Sneezy dust rose and settled. And there she stood behind the first act: my long-lost twin.

My heart pounded.

Memories crawled out of the tumult of my mind—the brutal *makukun* trainings, how we were forced to manifest supernatural power. And fight other children. Fight each other to death.

Now I was the blackened silhouette against the fire, and she was illuminated by its glow.

"I just wanted for us to see each other, to talk," I said stupidly.

"How quaint, that you wanted to talk," Kata said. She wore a royal-purple cloak, deep-set hood over her head, giving her that Grim Reaper impression. Even in the shadows I could still see her familial features, as the firelight danced in copper tones over her high cheekbones, and her eyes mirrored my own midnight-blue.

I was looking in a mirror. A fascinating, distorted mirror.

Except the scar. She doesn't wear my facial scar, because she was the one who cut me with the stick tip as a child. As accidents happen—honest, childhood, stick-sword-fighting accidents.

We were thinking the same thought.

Kata pulled back her hood as if she were brushing away a heavy cobweb. The fabric sloughed around her neck like dead skin. Her white hair flowed over her shoulders. Spiritual darkness pooled inside her eyes, almost a viscous substance, a soul having lost itself.

Her back bowed where mine straightened.

"*Sambalah* is gathering," she said. "The Dark Queen will rule these lands soon enough."

"Not if I do my job," I said.

Her lips pulled back, baring a flash of teeth. "If I do mine."

"I thought if you met me in person..." My voice faded. "Come with me to the Northern Peaks. It is never too late to change, to heal."

And then Kata didn't look quite human, in the manipulative orange firelight—she didn't look like the twin I remembered when we'd held each other, naked, latched in terror, feces ripe under our fingernails, sucking damp, mildewed pebbles to moisten our cracked throats, as horrid screams echoed in the catacombs outside our cell, not human, not even animal, and the splinters in our tongues scratched the roof of our mouths.

"I don't want you to choose the dark side," I shouted.

My bullwhip cracked. Black lightening. And Kata's legs flew out from under her, robes billowing as she body slammed onto the tavern floor.

The head knock sometimes makes that pumpkin sound. Knocks people unconscious.

This time it didn't.

Of course nothing is ever as simple as I want it to be.

I RUSHED OVER TO WHERE SHE HAD STOOD, STUMBLING OVER debris, and found only her heavy, empty robe. I gripped the soft material in my hand, felt her body heat.

"Kata," I screamed into the cavernous space. I spun in a circle, disoriented in the dark. "We can leave here together, go to the healers. People with medicines—soul medicines. They will cleanse your wounds, purge out the disease. You can find your soul and the higher path like I did. Please, I beg you. Please come with me."

"Never."

"But I came back for you that night," I shouted. "I ran back into the domiciles, searching and screaming for you and you weren't there in the catacombs, either. Not in the ossuary. I tried!"

"You left me." Her voice echoed from every direction, a haunting reverberation.

I tripped over a vessel. Inhaled a fruity, alcoholic wash of fig wine that twisted my stomach into a knot.

"I didn't mean to leave you," I called out. "I just wanted to escape the cult. Escape the rituals. I couldn't do it anymore, I couldn't hurt people, can't you understand that?"

The huge fire crackled and roared like a banshee.

Then I heard laughter dribbling in a corner, a thin snicker, growing louder, streaming out like the soft ooze of insanity.

That laughter, that vocal trill; she needled deeper into my head with that trill than a million splinters ever could.

The hard slap of reality hit me. She was mocking me. Playing my guilty conscience.

Because she had none.

"Oh, my poor, poor twin," Kata said, still lurking in the shadows. "I lured you here to kill you, and you just want to talk."

But I thought I heard jealousy in her voice. I thought I heard regret.

"I loved you," I whispered. "I still do."

"Fool. I ran away from you," she said. "Mother and I escaped through the sewers, along with the others."

Silence grew between us.

I agreed with her. Fool is right. I am good-intentioned but stupid.

The engorged fire billowed out with a *whoosh,* drawing my attention. The logs shifted. The glow brightened.

Look, it said. Look around you at the truth.

Slowly, softly, my mind allowed me to become aware of the piled-up ring of dead bodies encircling me. The bodies had all been previously shuffled just outside the illumination of the firelight. A grotesque perimeter.

A horrid death count.

More horrid than I had realized.

Severed torsos, guts distended. Limbs jacked up like jigsaw pieces that would never connect again.

I stood, boots soaked in a river of blood.

There would be no survivors posse on its way.

Everyone was dead.

I closed my eyes. I focused my Qi and called upon a brilliant, spiritual shield. It rose around me in a golden glow. Evil gets all extravagant and love is just simple. As a hutsu, my shield is the only supernatural ability I use.

Kata screamed in demonic fury.

She tried to kill me with every supernatural thing she had. Some evil people get too mentally sick in this world to ever choose to heal.

I knew nightmares would plague me for months.

My bullwhip took her life.

I CARRIED HER BODY IN MY SHAKING ARMS, GENTLY TO THE edge of the fire.

The rabid heat scorched my skin.

I kissed her face in the wild glow. Her skin stuck to my lips for a moment.

My tears rained into her lifeless, midnight-blue eyes—and spilled out again over her own cheeks. With my palms I kindly swept her eyelids closed. I brushed her long white hair back with my shaking fingers. Her hair felt brittle. I thought: I wish I could have shared my moisturizer with you. Because we have our mother's wiry hair.

The Dark Queen.

And you were your mother's daughter.

And I am not.

I said *I'm sorry* over and over.

When I looked up, the fire was almost out. Just coals glaring at me with red, pulsing eyes.

In the dark, I found the liquid accelerant.

I ESCAPED THE ROILING GRAY SMOKE THAT CHASED ME OUT, hurrying over the wobbly tavern door, taking a big gulp of fresh, apple-fragranced air—the same passageway I'd come in, but I would never be the same again

Komb, the giant dwarf, stood easy across the dirt road.

He blended into the layers of shadow—his familiar outline leaning against an enormous oak tree, his thick arms folded across his broad chest, as gnarled and cantankerous as the bark. His ax blade gleamed in a crescent moon grin along with his one good eye, narrowed, which reflected the raging blaze of the monstrous crematorium behind me.

I'd never been so grateful to see him. I'd never felt so ashamed.

I tried to hurry across the dusty road, but my limp came back suddenly, a sharp catch of pain in the hip socket. It shortens my gait.

Step-hobble. Step-hobble.

I thought about the paralytic sweetbark.

It took a hundred years to reach the other side of the road.

"Didn't swallow it," he said. "And I followed ya. We've all had ta do it, Wynd. Had ta face the evil of our bloodlines any way we know how. And I don't take no offense."

A flood of gratitude for Komb's acceptance flushed my whole body, a tidal wave of relief. I thought it might carry me down to the ground, but I stood.

I caught the flicker of the sandcat's back-and-forth tail, loyal beside Komb's chest, punishing the air, her fur the color of stormy sky and stern disapproval. Probably an apology to the wild beast would take more time.

"That was a hard one for ya, Wynd. We give them the choice, we can't make 'em change. You get it done?"

I knew he was asking, *Did I kill the witch?* I started to say, *She's dead,* but I choked on the smallest amount of saliva, and the words strangled up into a strange sound.

So I nodded, *Yes.*

I looked up at the sky. My tears fell back into my ears, drawing spirals.

"It's parta the hutsu path." Komb's voice softened. "It's multigenerational evil we're trying ta clean up here. An evil don't want ta do right."

I bit my upper lip for comfort. But all the salt was gone. Only the bitter taste of sorrow and ash.

"Can you imagine these lands if no one did nothing? They'd usher in a demonic hell. They may do it, anyway."

A wind picked up. Tossed leaves and smelled like pine sap. Fed the blaze.

"We'll go back to the Northern Peaks now. Back ta

where you can rest and heal and find peace again with it." Komb turned his attention away from me, intrigued. "Much as the fire is burning, it's all contained. Won't spread ta the countryside."

I looked back over my shoulder. Black wood hissed and popped in a volcanic red embrace, a blaze that would consume everything, leaving only a pile of smoldering rubble under the sun's first morning rays.

Ash and bones.

Bones and memories.

"Late-night travelers rolled a cart wheel up the eastern route." He laid his gaze on my face again. "But they'll be round about here again soon. We best be gone. My horse is down the hill in the orchard with yours."

It was impossible to tell, but I think he winked at me.

We walked together. The fragrance of new apples. Crickets chittering. The snap of twigs breaking under our feet.

"I left a note for our comrades before I took chase a' ya, and they'll meet us at Red Castle. We'll have a healing circle for you, Wynd. You'll be okay. We won't leave 'til you feel right ta travel again. You were a tortured child, 'member that. We all were. We understand."

I don't know what came over me then. I reached out and took his hand. I took the wind out of that giant dwarf; he lost his breath for a step or two, I could tell.

His hand was warm as baked bread, rough as coral stone.

He squeezed me back.

"I don't want friends," I whispered.

Komb scoffed; that deep, loving rumble he makes. I almost smiled.

I folded the sound up and put it safe in my heart to mend where it was broken. I'm a hutsu hunter. The Dark Queen was rising.

Now I knew who she was and what I would do.

SKINWALKER

DREW THREW the can of soda with her softball pitcher's arm at the wall of her grandfather's mud-colored adobe house. It exploded with a *bang* and the fizzy clear liquid sprayed up into the hot, deep blue sky of the Albuquerque desert like a crystal chandelier fractured by a shotgun.

A fine misty rainbow plumed around her and fell to the caked dirt of a backyard, smelling sweet like fry bread. Drew got even madder because it was so flipping hot outside and she'd wanted a cold drink.

Now she didn't have one anymore.

This pueblo really looked like it was made out of mud just dug right out of the ground, all smoothed out by the builders' hands as they rounded the edges, shiny square glass windows reflecting the big sun with buttery copper winks, and the roof flat as a tortilla.

It was all ancient Indian ruins meets designer New York architect—or something like that. Except the dirt yard was strewn with junky odds and ends, like that rusty truck bumper and an upside down ceramic bathroom sink.

The heat of the late afternoon sun irritated her neck where tender skin was newly exposed. Her long black hair had been damaged in the car fire, singed off actually, on the right side. So she'd fixed the problem herself. Buzzed the back with Dad's clippers while she was still in Chicago last week, scissored the sides for a girly, feminine 'hawk but, well—that didn't work out.

So basically she looked like she could join the military now, a fourteen-year-old, and she had the muscled arms to prove it.

Maybe people would leave her alone.

Not that anybody had said anything yet out here in the middle of roadrunner nowhere, except the taxi cab driver, who'd said good luck. He'd also plucked that Sprite out of a little Styrofoam cooler, complete with a palm print stain in dried ketchup on the lid, and tossed the can out his passenger's window.

Drew hadn't expected the throw, had glanced up at the streaking sun and blinded out, but she'd still caught the drink.

Because you want to play the ball, don't let it play you.

Her grandfather on her dad's side, whom she'd never met, was supposed to be home but he wasn't. And the taxi cab had vanished along the stupid dirt road that led back to the city, that just shot off along the flat mesa and the dried bushes in a straight line, and left her here in nowheresville.

Just a cloud of dust like a phantom train disappearing

until no trace was left. She watched the dust fade all the way back to clear sky.

And Mom had taken Drew's cell phone before she'd boarded the private jet.

Because no one can know where you are. No one, do you understand, honey? Not until the attack gets sorted out. You can't text your friends. You can't trust your friends anymore. We can't even trust the police.

I won't text my friends.

You will.

The melted plastic taste came back, coating the roof of her mouth, like the car fire was happening all over again. She pushed the memory of that midnight event outside the Lincolnworth Club away because in reality it was bright and hot here.

Here was not *there*. It was not *then*.

Drew walked up to the home's southern facing wall in her Gucci rubber flip-flops, where the dripping soda had darkened on the clay and started to look like one of those inkblot Rorschach tests, you know—the kind that the psychs use to test for crazy people.

Or that you can do with your friends online.

She squat down to pick up the busted green can, her too-tight jeans baring her butt crack again, which was really getting on her nerves all today—from sitting cross-legged on the bed in the private jet, chasing the sun in the western sky, and then hurrying through the airways of the Albuquerque International Sunport with the address her mom had scrawled on a Post-It note.

Why did she have to grab this pair out of the walk-in closet instead of her Forever denim?

And who calls an airport a sunport?

She glanced over her tight pink T-shirted shoulder—across the tumbleweed yard, over a crumpled up blue tarp, and beyond the decaying edges of a cinderblock wall. The air smelled like sagebrush and squeezed lime.

The great yawning wasteland was a National Geographic photograph she didn't even want to be in.

This was the Isleta Pueblo reservation. The very northern edge, where Indian switched over to White Man on the map, right? Her dad had grown up in Albuquerque. Could this be his childhood home? She didn't even know. Dad didn't talk childhood.

Zero cars in the driveway, zero grandpa answering the front door even though she had knocked for like five minutes after the taxi left.

No neighbors except the sunbathing lizards she'd seen doing pushups on the big boulder by the front door.

Oh yeah, and that shaggy black, long-legged dog jumping over the broken fence as she'd handed the twenties over to the taxi man from the back seat. Must've been scared off.

Drew wiped off the sand stuck to the fizzing, hissing Sprite can and sucked the cool-tasting sugar water out of the split in the container between the capital S and the lowercase P.

The sharp aluminum threatened to cut her dry tongue.

She stood up, crumpling the can a little more in her fist, then dropping it.

The giant fireball of a sun was sinking to the west way out there beyond the purple-tinted hills, where maybe it looked a little like it could be the end of the world, too.

Shadows were beginning a steady crawl across the pockmarked ground, lengthening and stretching and every moment maybe a little darker.

Okay fine.

No iPhone. No long-lost grandfather named Rick. No other choice. It was time to go into the house because what else was she supposed to do? Sit on her suitcase until a rattlesnake strolled up and fanged her on the butt?

She retraced her steps across the gravelly driveway to her White Sox overnight bag and slung it over her shoulder.

I don't want to go to New Mexico, Mom. Don't make me go.

I've got to hide you somewhere, Drew.

But Dad is estranged and doesn't want me to meet to his father, ever. He'll be so mad. I'm not allowed to talk about that side of the family, don't you understand anything?

I understand plenty, you little brat. Watch your mouth. Your grandfather Rick is just a nothing-old medicine man, he's agreed you can stay for a few days. No one will think to look for you there.

You can't make me go.

I will.

The front entry to the house was a red arch with a blue painted door. A few wooden splinters waited patiently on the door frame to cactus-poke the next finger that came near. A spiky plant brushed Drew's wrist.

Instead of knocking over and over this time, she

pushed down the iron latch on the door and it opened like it had no defense.

It's not breaking in if it just opens, right?

"Hello, " she called. A refreshing, floral rush of air exhaled over her face. "Rick?"

Her flip-flops smacked her heels as she stepped through the threshold and set the bag on a stone-cut floor with a thunk. She closed the door behind her.

Then it was all silent. A thick, gathering silence.

Kinda like the silence of being unwelcome.

Drew just stood there, feeling the flow of uncertainty squeeze through her chest, thickening within her arms and legs, pooling in her feet like a hardening glue.

She didn't want to walk further into the house and she didn't want to go back outside.

"Rick?" But of course she knew no one was home.

In the last rays of buttery light fading through the windows, Drew saw the interior walls of the house were rounded and arched in pinkish-coral adobe. Quaint little southwestern style decor—a wool blanket with a kachina doll hung from an iron rack on the wall, a clay pot on a coffee table with red hand-blown glass chilies, shelves with those miniature cactuses.

But the couches and chairs were covered with ghostly white sheets.

Like the kind you put up when you're on a long vacation.

Beyond the living room, the northern face of a clean kitchen poked its nose around the corner, the view of the desert sky through a high round window looked like a wise woman's worried eye, the black iris of night dilating.

The inside of this house said female touch all over it.

Yes, and it even smelled faintly like lavender, or a woman's perfume. And Drew's mom had said her grandfather lived *alone*. And no offense to her Dad and all, but genetically he wouldn't know how to decorate or cook or perfume anything if it could save him a punch in the face.

The light kept draining out of the windows.

Drew took a few steps closer to a collection of photographs on a bookshelf full of worn paperbacks. They were all white people.

Every single one.

Drew felt her stomach clench. Dad didn't talk childhood, but he wasn't white. His skin was even darker than Drew's.

Two sharp knocks pounded against the door behind her back.

Drew whirled around, her hands in the defensive position like the batter had smacked a chopper at her face. But she didn't have a glove. She wasn't fast pitching on the mound.

And who knocks on their own front door?

Only the hiss of her flip-flops scuffing as she had turned. Only her eyes flitting to the unlocked iron latch inches away.

And no peephole.

Her heart pounded, raw and offbeat. A terrible feeling crawled down her spine—the feeling of danger. The feeling of malevolence.

Her ears were scanning like radar, trying to hear anything.

She softly pressed both hands on the door, then her foot against the doorjamb, feeling for a vibration, like she could keep the barrier from swinging open, because she hadn't seen a splash of headlights on the walls, hadn't heard car tires crunching gravel, hadn't heard a car door slam.

No one should be outside but someone was.

And it wasn't a normal someone.

Drew wanted to call her mom and say help me. And then Drew thought, what is wrong with me, just say hello, just say hello who's there?

Instead, she flipped the lock with a loud *ker-clunk.*

It echoed like a public confession.

She took one step away from the door, wishing she could grip the steel of her Beretta. Dad hid the firearms behind the false wall in the basement. Mom didn't let her go down there but she did anyway.

There wasn't another knock, or even a fleck of a sound like a leaf scratching.

Drew took a few more steps backward in her flip-flops and they smacked her heels because they are the noisiest shoes a person can wear.

She tried to scoot her feet instead. *Shhhhh,* her flip-flops cried.

Drew left them behind.

Her toes widened on the smooth stone, squished on the soft plush carpet, pattered across the linoleum, as she retreated backward until she bumped the kitchen table with her thigh.

Her hand squeezed the sticky wooden frame on the back of a chair. Released. Squeezed again.

Her shallow exhale pooled under her nose, smelled like stomach acid.

In the dim light there was an L-shaped counter and double sink and upright cupboards. Drew searched for the elongated shape of a cordless phone on the counter. The oven clock said eight forty-five in neon green. *Mom, I need you.* And a light switch?

The dim border of a sliding glass door frame pinned and stretched the blue-black skin of the night, tattooed with sickly yellow stars.

Why did you have to start a divorce?

Because your father's a cocksucker.

No he's not, you're the one who sucks cock.

And Mom had backslapped Drew right then, in the aqua-blue Porsche Cayman idling at a red light, in the middle of downtown Chicago with a full crosswalk of suits streaming by carrying their dead animal briefcases, answering their calls with shiny perfect teeth because it was all too important to wait. And Drew remembered how mom's Maurice Lacroix watch had scratched Drew's jaw with a thin mark that somehow looked like the letter C. How her long hair had stuck to the line of salty sweat on her upper lip—where the slap started swelling, just a little.

Then Drew snapped back to reality.

This wasn't Illinois.

And now she was crouched behind the legs of the kitchen table and chairs, peering through them like cell bars, hiding from the thugs her mega-bucks attorney dad kept around whenever the bar was an open bar, like the rowdy pool parties, the World Series BBQ's. Because he was one of the suits. A dirty suit. Her family was crime money and she knew it.

No one ever had to tell her. It was what you learned by example.

Drew's palms were drenched in sweat.

Dr. Lahoya had said that when the PTSD starts, Drew was supposed to try and get her nervous system to go back to its normal state.

To find the trigger and remove it.

But now Mom was going all states evidence and Drew had been subpoenaed, too. Was served last week. Just before the car accident—the car *bomb*.

Drew's pitching hand flitted up to her neck to pull her hair out of her face, but there was no hair there anymore. She kept forgetting that. The stubs were rough and scratchy. She wanted her long, blue-black ponytail. Why had she cut it off? That was stupid.

Everything was stupid.

A weak crescent moon drooped like it was pinned up in the sky by a single thumbtack. Okay, just stand up. Just walk around fast and flick on every single light in the house and find a phone.

"You can do this," she whispered to herself and her own voice sounded like someone else.

A figure moved across the backyard, between the mounded blue tarp and the horizontal cinderblock wall.

Drew peered out through the sliding glass doors with scalpel eyes. It was hard to see.

It was a black-on-black shadow oozing out of the pores of the night like a pool of ink, tall and lurking, and then Drew recognized the huge front paws of a dog, the hump of a knotted neck and muscled shoulders.

That same black dog. She'd seen it jumping over the cinderblocks in the sun earlier.

Now the huge dog pawed across the dirty yard, up onto the concrete patio, and pressed its fat pinkish nose to the glass. It's nostrils flared like a pig, the tip bending, drawing a smear mark. Making an elongated squeak.

It drew a Z. Looking left, then down, then right. Then straight at her.

It had an extra long neck.

Bloodshot red eyes, like dried ketchup. Like the ketchup on the taxi man's cooler when he'd tossed the soda. And for an irrational second Drew thought the dog had eaten the taxi man, and now his soul was trapped inside.

She'd been *with* the taxi man when she first saw the dog.

Paying him the money.

To leave her here. The address on the PostIt.

Which someone had switched.

An overwhelming stink of rotten eggs washed over Drew and she gagged on stomach acid. Her eyes were on the dog, she couldn't look away. Couldn't even blink.

His lips pulled back, shiny white teeth except they were a man's set of teeth, straight and perfect and pearly white.

"Mouth shut," the dogman's voice gurgled like its throat was full of liquid. "Keep it."

He slowly rose up, stood up on his long, sinewy legs and he was an ungodly eight feet tall, the red eyes angled down at Drew and she almost started to pee herself but she clenched her abdomen tight.

The dog man coughed and chunks of meat and blood sprayed the window. Drew screamed until she ran out of sound. The cry rang in her ears. The fleshy chunks clung, slid, and then fell with a faint plopping sound onto the concrete patio.

Drew's lungs couldn't inhale.

They were flat.

The dogman dropped to his forepaws, his neck hairs spiked and agitated, the hide itself readjusting over flesh like ripples on a lake. In the dark shadows the cheekbones shifted, a man's grimace now seething, a dog's snout now snarling with yellow canine fangs.

Then the creature squat low and jumped high, landing with a four-footed thump on the roof.

The jaundiced moon still hung there, far out in space, a child's paper cutout about to fall off its tack. Drew's right arm, the one her upper body was leaning on, began to shake violently. She dropped to her elbows on the kitchen linoleum.

Crawled like a worm cut in two, the upper body flinching forward in the dark.

Phone, she thought. Phone.

She drug herself to the counter.

Stand, she thought. Stand up.

She got to her knees, got crouched on her bare feet. Reached up and felt the cool, dry ceramic sink under her sweaty, slick palms. Then she vomited nothing but air there. Her brain was commanding her hands to fumble with the drawers and open them fast, *bang* went silverware clattering onto the floor everywhere, but Drew gripped a butcher knife in her shaking hand.

Dimly, a pale light switch on the opposite wall pointed at her like a slender finger beckoning.

Drew ran forward. A fork stabbed her arch.

With each step the fork jabbed deeper into her foot but she limped fast until she flicked the switch and a chandelier blew the kitchen up in bright white.

Drew whirled in every direction. She was in a fish bowl now, unable to see beyond her own reflection in all the glass windows.

No dogman inside.

Drew's looked up, her eyes probing the ceiling. Up there.

And now she finally took a deep breath. Convulsed for air actually, her ribs swelling. She yanked the fork out of her arch.

The butcher knife clutched in front of her body with one hand, Drew hurried down a hallway and pushed open a plain brown door, fumbled for a light switch, flooded the next room with color, ran around a quilted bed, stubbed her big toe in a stab of brilliant pain and dove at the nightstand, knocking over the golden lamp which clanged to the floor.

The cordless phone glowed in numeric red. She punched 911 and got nothing.

No, no, no. She punched 911 and got nothing again.

Fuck.

The room smelled like fake peaches.

Something brushed the window behind the closed brown curtains. Now something scratched the glass. Drew backed away, back into the hall. She ran to the far end, passing dark entryways, diving again toward a light switch which bombed another room into color.

All the nooks and crannies of a stranger's home and it was a twisted labyrinth.

From far away, in the other universe of the house, Drew distinctly heard the front door unlocking with the same loud *ker-clunk.*

A chipped blue tiled countertop. Purple gardening shoes. Rusty stacked tools.

Drew lurched around rows of green foliage and terra-cotta pots to a door leading outside and it was locked. The scream just rolled up inside her, exploding out through her mouth as her one free hand shook and shook and shook the knob like maybe if she could express her feelings enough it might magically allow her though.

Rotate the button, her brain commanded.

Rotate the button, her brain repeated.

Drew stopped. She looked down at her hand white-knuckled and death-latched on the round doorknob.

Oh, she just had to turn the thingy in the center.

So she turned the thingy and the door opened wide and a warm wash of high desert air welcomed her into the folds of twisted shadow and tormented shape.

Wait, that was a car.

Parked just five feet from her, right there, for real. The

light from the hallway streamed out and reflected on the bumper of a gray Camry, and the license plate said New Mexico Land Of Enchantment.

The north side of the house. She hadn't checked the north side? No, she hadn't.

There are keys on the blue counter, her brain said.

There are keys on the counter, her brain repeated.

Drew ran back and got the keys, fired up the engine, and peeled out like a banshee. The tires kicked up dirt and rocks, splintering a window behind her.

Her headlights cut through the night like swords, slicing the dirt road into pie-shaped yellow wedges and all else was black. She shot forward like a spaceship on warp drive, nothing else but the streaking stars above. The instrument panel hemorrhaged red. Drew raced across washboard bumps that chattered her teeth. Delicate objects bounced and tinker-belled and then shattered to silence in the backseat.

The butcher knife gleamed. Pinned to the steering wheel.

In the rearview, the huge dogman kept pace with the car. His wide legs swallowed each galloping stride.

She floored it.

A notebook slid across the dashboard with a hiss. The glove compartment snapped open and its guts tumbled out.

The dogman was gone in the rearview, but then Drew turned her head and saw him again. Racing seventy miles-per-hour alongside the Camry, the dogman's bones cracked and reset anew just a few feet from her closed window, rippling like the hide itself might fall off and leave only skinned, dog-shaped raw muscles rhythmically pumping through the shadows.

But the fur cloak thing hung on.

This time Drew could not scream.

There were no screams left.

She spun the wheel and broadsided the evil beast. The sickening metal-to-flesh collision dented her door inward. The knife shot up toward her face and she ducked before it slit her neck. In the moment while Drew spun off the road, to the south in the distance, she saw an orange glow.

The dying coals of a campfire.

She spun back onto the dirt road, Hawaii Five-O'ed a ditch and smacked her head on the roof and kept her foot floored all the way until the tires crossed civilized pavement and she shot through an intersection on a red light like a space capsule on emergency reentry.

THE REST OF THE NIGHT WAS A BLUR AT THE ALBUQUERQUE police department, wrapped up in a white cotton blanket that smelled like bleach, going through the recorded interviews with the female detectives, two cups of coffee and a hot chocolate staining empty Styrofoam cups, and also a half-eaten day-old sandwich—until she met her grandfather.

And then the night came into focus.

He stood in the doorframe, just about as big as it with his detective uniform on, and when he said Drew's name for the first time her whole body broke out in goosebumps. When she looked up she knew she'd recognize his dancing eyes anywhere.

On any face.

Because kindred souls have a connection like that.

He explained that he'd been briefed about everything.

Other cops were walking by, their leather belts making that groaning sound, and phones were ringing and conversations carrying.

"Come with me where it's quiet," he said. And he stood back so respectfully to give her the space to come out of the door.

Still barefoot. Blanket ends trailing.

They went up to the roof and sat at a secret smokers' table. There was a glass ashtray. The moon and stars seemed more like the dome of a planetarium over the city, and the show was just beginning.

They talked and laughed a little out of nervousness and then the natural comfort grew between their difference in age and made a bridge between them.

"I thought you lived out on a reservation," she said. "I googled it and I thought you were Pueblo. Mom said you were like a traditional, uh—Indian shaman or something."

Rick smiled, the lights around the building softening the lines on his sixty-year-old face. "The detective part went undetected."

The city lights blurred in reds and yellows and green.

He crinkled a wrapper off a red-and-white peppermint candy. "What do you know about your heritage?" he asked, popping the candy slowly into his mouth.

"I'm Italian," Drew said. "My Mom's Italian." She felt her cheeks start to burn.

Rick nodded. The candy poked around in his cheek. Clanked on his teeth. "I understand what you mean." He turned his gaze to look out the window from the high rise and Drew looked out there, too.

Drew tried to pull her hair back again and there was no hair there anymore. She folded her hands on the table.

Her grandfather's amazingly warm hand slid over her knuckles. Their skin touched. His palm didn't have any calluses.

"I wasn't allowed to ask about you, ever," she said. "I found one black-and-white photo of you once, and Dad took it from me. He was mad."

"He had a lot to be mad about in the Four Corners growing up," Rick said. "There's a deep family history on the rez out there—between your uncles. You're Dine, did you know that, Drew? Navajo?"

"Not Pueblo?"

"Not Pueblo."

The city lights kaleidoscoped, twisting and fracturing. The first tear in her eye fell across her cheek. It burned with a longing she couldn't find words for.

They sat at the table, holding hands.

She felt safe.

"The Chicago scandal just hit the international news this evening," Rick said. "I took a call, your Dad is in jail. Mom is going into protective custody. They're giving you that option too until the trial is over. Or you can stay with a family member—with me, if you'd like. I can fly back to Chicago to help you get your things."

Another tear fell. This one splashed by the ashtray.

Her life was split apart. Fractured. Everything she'd ever known in Chicago was gone.

Drew pulled her hand but her grandfather held on. She looked up into his eyes and he had glistening tears on his cheeks, too.

"What happened?" They both knew she wasn't asking about what happened in Chicago. "I reported it was a man who attacked me, I didn't want to say the rest. But what *was* it?"

"Chicago hired a Skinwalker to scare you. So you won't testify against your father. Or about what you witnessed up there."

Drew felt ice cold though the night was warm. She pulled the blanket tighter.

"Hey, you're safe now." Rick reached into his uniform and withdrew a little dark bottle. "It's cedar wood essential oil. Give it a few whiffs."

He set it on the table before her and the woody aroma calmed her.

"Best I can figure, they sent you to an empty house on five hundred acres of empty land so no one would witness the event. It's become a dark art. Didn't always used to be, not like this. But every native culture all over the world has a name for those who practice evil. Our brothers and sisters, taken by the lie. Even the white folk have their Necromancers." He glanced at Drew and winked. "Those Italians."

Drew wanted to hide but he squeezed her hand and she knew it was all okay.

"Secret clans," he continued. "They train in ceremony. They wear animal skins to transform. But we're the other side of the medicine, Drew. The good guys, if you chose it."

Then she knew why she'd always hated all the suits.

And hated moneyed Chicago.

Because they only helped themselves, the ruling class. And then they backstabbed each other, anyway. So what was the point? Wasn't a lesser evil still an evil?

And now it was suddenly crystal clear the moment she had first *known*. It was the first moment she had seen her Navajo grandfather's eyes all the way back when she was eight years old and had found that black-and-white photograph in the Burberry shoebox with the golden embossed knight.

The twinkling light from Rick's photographed eyes had reached out of the paper and touched her with rays like healing sun. Just like the warmth of his hand now, holding her cold fingers.

All the way back then—she *knew*. And she had made her choice, even if she forgot it later on, because life was hard.

Maybe she'd funneled all her hope into sports, hurling the fastest pitch in the state. And every time she threw the ball she was trying to break free from the darkness that bound her.

And Dad had seen all that when she was only nine, and

had taken the photograph and tore it up into pieces and laughed as he pointed a Beretta at her face.

You'll work for me, bright eyes.

Sometimes crime gets in the way.

But not anymore.

STING GIRL

ON TUESDAY the national news announced it was a World War again, by Thursday all the Chronics had been rounded up from their San Francisco homes and apartments, and sometime in the middle of a pitch black Saturday night Trinity Jane Nickelfire finally stumbled from a monster-green Army transport truck and was herded by drones into a medical camp by bright, blinding lights.

Now, she lay like a broken China doll on a damp patch of dirt, shivering under a piss-brown tarp, trying to keep her twitching muscles from jumping out of her skin.

The tarp crinkled like birthday wrapping paper.

It was annoying.

When she'd finally fallen asleep, she'd even had a stupid birthday dream where her mom and dad were singing in a sunny yellow kitchen and everybody was all excited, the lemon poppy-seed cake had seventeen candles, and then *bam!* the cake blew up and her parents ran around screaming with blood spurting from their flesh-peeled faces.

Bacterial nightmares were a drag.

When you woke up you really quick had to count ten good things that you knew were true. When you were done counting, the lies in the nightmare would already be fading away.

Because for one, she'd never known her real parents, so they weren't going to lose their faces.

And secondly, she couldn't eat sugar anymore. So any kind of cake was like broccoli and she didn't miss it.

Not when sugar made her symptoms worse.

Trinity realized suddenly her neuro twitch had stopped. She held her breath under the tarp. Even the low-grade buzzing vibrations under her skin were gone.

It was always a freaking miracle when her infected body went still.

She almost smiled. But it was too much work.

A coughing fit punctured the night. That same phlegmy lung-hacker from inside the Army-green blowup tent had started up with his whoop again. Damn mucous-filled stranger, laying there inside that sea of metallic folding cots with the other parchment-paper-faced people gripping their woolen blankets under the glow of blue service lights (that made everyone look like they were wearing black mascara)—*hack, hack, hack.*

The terrified whispers. The uncontrolled moans. The *psst* escape of stinky cabbage farts—then *hack, hack, hack.*

But really it was the cabbage farts that had been too much. Who could breathe?

Within the first hour after arrival, Trinity had dropped out of her cot and crawled secretly along the modular plastic floor of the Army tent on her hands and knees.

Just to find fresh air somewhere.

The hexagonal floor pieces had been snapped together like a jigsaw puzzle and the little drainage holes had pinched circular imprints into her palms. Trinity had slunk past one row of pot-bellied cots and then another. The tall folks with their feet dangling. Cold blue toes.

Her bony knees spiked with pain through moss-green drawstring pants—the identical bottoms they'd all been issued with white T-shirt tops.

Trinity had thought the spherical nurse drones would track her movement at the canvass exit flaps, but for some reason the ocular sensors didn't sense her.

The nurse drones had panels that could open, and all kinds of medical gadgets could extend on mechanical probes. Each drone had a different numeric identifier and a barcode. They floated down the rows, smooth white basketballs with a big red plus sign, monitoring their human horde.

While Trinity had crawled secretly away.

Technology was stupid.

The tracking frequency of Trinity's V2 identity chip must have been malfunctioning. She'd investigated the digital tattoo, permanently flush to the skin on her wrist. Tapped the touch screen, but it had just glared darkly at her with a singular white pixel. That was unusual. In fact, the device had never blinked with a single white square before.

She should have made a break for it then. Run like hell and escaped. But who could run? She hadn't even felt like her legs could stand.

Instead, she had collapsed under this piss-brown tarp just outside the Army tent (what a lame escape)—and now the fresh air probed through the holes in the plastic with cold, airy fingers.

Fragrant and clean and wild, blowing in from somewhere that couldn't possibly be another stinking city, the intoxicating, honey-sweet breeze could have been funneled right through the perfume section of an elite consortium.

You know what?

It smelled gorgeous.

Where the hell had the military stashed her, anyway? She'd never been in a targeted group before—not through any of the world wars in her brief stint of life so far. She wasn't a member of a disapproved religion, she wasn't Anti-Technology, she was just a plain old teenager of the Latina variety.

And inside the melting pot of The City, Latina was still cool.

Trinity ground her teeth. It was having an incurable disease that wasn't cool.

It was having to fear your own government that wasn't cool.

For most of Trinity's life the domestic terrorist attacks

had been cranking up to an insane level. Finally, the defense conglomerates had run for President under the state of emergency *Save Our Sovereignty* campaigns, and the question had been fervently debated—how *do* we save the country?

The pundits squawked while domestic terrorists blew more stuff up. Bye-bye Golden Gate Bridge. There was a national vote. The defense corporations officially merged into one corporation and the new Universal One became the first elected Corporate President.

Save Our Sovereignty had become the final answer.

The end to capitalism would allow the release of scientific patents that had been keep secret for centuries. New technology would save us from the terrorists who had sacked Washington. The state. (Because Washington D.C. would have been too much).

Reality changed overnight.

It was like a science fiction movie except it wasn't a movie.

Nanobots in the sky to fix global warming, made-to-order cloned organs, a new central digital monetary system with digital tattoos (everybody has to have one), and these UFO flying disc things that all along had existed.

Free energy boxes called the Free-E Device hit the shelves. Google already had the hover car.

But Chronic disease.

It was poking a dangerous hole right through all the political lies.

Trinity never should have told her doctors anything.

And she should have kept trying to hide her symptoms from her foster mother. She'd punched her ticket to this quarantine camp (Oh excuse me, I mean *medical facility)* with that fateful blood draw. But how was she supposed to know World War Whatever was just around the corner? That the rumors about Chronic disease being a biological weapon against its own people were going to get all mainstream and in everybody's face?

The muscles in her forearm started twisting like angry snakes again.

The bacterial infections under her skin were winning their own world war—hijacking her nerves. Her immune system lost the battle a little more every day.

She was dying, but she couldn't die. It was like your own body turned into a torture chamber and you couldn't get out.

But she was still trying to stay positive. Out here in the night. But the nightmare feelings started pulling her down like an anchor to the bottom of a drowning sea.

That stranger's hacking cough. *Hack, hack, hack.*

Just stop coughing.

Please stop coughing.

I hate you when you cough.

She'd had enough of that sound. Trinity yanked the tarp off her body. The cold sky goose-bumped her skin. The moon hung sickly, a clawing fingernail losing its grip on reality. The weak stars were swollen, bloated eyes.

She would try running anyway, after all. Maybe find the perimeter and sneak out and hitchhike her way back to San Francisco and live, where?—on the streets?

Hack, hack, hack the cougher laughed. I'm *sick, sick, sick* and so are you.

Screw running, Trinity thought. Screw all the healthy people who can still run. Vertigo swooped down on her, like she was dropping through the ground continually, without end.

She hated that symptom.

She needed help. She couldn't lay here forever. She needed to be warm.

Trinity took as deep a breath as she could, and then just went ahead and screamed—*Screw you Universal One, you're trying to take over the world you lying sacks of shit, you created this disease to weaken your own people*—as loud as she could.

It was totally exhausting.

If her V2 was still malfunctioning, she would be undetectable and off the grid as long as she was unseen and quiet. But nothing would call a police drone on a her ass faster than a good ol' domestic terrorist diatribe.

Which she'd just given.

The menacing and low mechanical whir of a Three-Point Tactical Drone shot up within twelve inches of her nose, its mirrored black helmet-head on a long, telescoping neck. The shoulders and retractable arms were Herculean. It was the creepiest flying robot ever made. A marriage between a grey alien and an African boomslang snake. No legs. It struck like lightening and was weaponized.

A red laser sliced across Trinity's eyes in a microsecond, reading her retinas for identification with a bright stab of pain.

(After Universal One came into power, everybody had

one month to get their retinas scanned at the DMV. The wait lines were horrific.) The drone's handcuff lashed out and gripped Trinity's upper arm like amputation might be a frequent side effect. She was yanked painfully up to her feet.

Well, it was too cold outside, anyway. And she shouldn't be laying on the dirt while she was fighting an infection.

Maybe solitary confinement would be warmer. Quieter, too. She'd spent the last year and a half lying in bed, anyway.

At least when she was alone it wouldn't smell like one hundred other people's digestive issues.

Solitary smelled blank, if blank can be a smell.

It was too quiet and that made the tinnitus in her ears worse. Like hearing nonstop dual tones. And the glaring blueish-white lights inside the ceiling panels never went off. Even when she closed her eyes—blue.

An indestructible camera observed her with a shiny glass lens in a corner. Even during the night when she had those screaming nightmares where people blew up, and the panic and anxiety coiled around her ribs like a constricting snake trying to swallow her for days on end, the camera just watched.

Like a one-eyed voyeur.

The claustrophobic white walls were cubical, the

temperature was neutral, and she lived under a scratchy wool blanket on a spongy plastic floor mat with a metal ration food bowl and water cup as her only friends. They were filled twice a day. When shoved through a slat in the wall onto a conveyor belt they both said *shmmmm.*

A black-and-white instruction panel bolted on the wall next to the conveyor belt kindly informed in twelve languages: RETURN VESSELS TO RECEPTACLE. NO EXCEPTIONS.

Corporate One's logo—a little blue rectangle with the left side missing, just like a backward, block letter C—emblazoned nearly everything. Like somebody in marketing couldn't figure out this wasn't the best place to advertise the brand.

A hole in the ground vaporized her bodily functions.

That was kinda cool. Every house should have one.

When Trinity was awake she really missed her cell phone and the internet. Cut off from contact with the outside world, she longed for the feel of her smooth leather phone case snug in her palm. At least now her foster mother couldn't call her up and yell.

Trinity would fall asleep and when she woke up she had all these same thoughts again.

Try having a chronic brain infection.

It's a trip.

It really is like your thoughts erase over and over, then you discover them anew.

A paper cup with useless pink pills accompanied every meal. She tossed the drugs in the vaporizer. The mirrored camera didn't seem to care either way.

Was anybody even watching the feed?

She rode the constant wave of symptoms. *Twitch, twitch, twitch.* The same symptoms that had been explained and debated on the national news before the World War was announced—fever, night sweats, joint pain, crazy-weird neurological stuff, fatigue, sound sensitivity, seizures—oh, and don't forget the short-term memory loss.

Did she say that already?

It's like every day becomes the same day, without the day before.

On the national news, right before the World War was announced, a bunch of famous people had just started going public about being diagnosed with Chronic. Actors couldn't finish shooting the movie. Congress folks getting confused at law meetings. People falling away out of society.

Where were they? In bed.

And they were suffering. No two doctors alike could agree on treatment. Except treatments often failed.

So when the famous folks started asking what this chronic disease really was, and where it came from, and why there was a cover-up of the epidemic?—Well, those were innocent questions. And that was probably going to be a problem.

For the folks.

Who weren't so innocent.

A SOLDIER IN ARMY FATIGUES OPENED TRINITY'S DOOR IN THE wall. She hadn't seen a real person in a long time—how long? Her inability to track time made her feel crazy.

The soldier was young and cute and patriotic but his eyes didn't smile.

Trinity's legs held her up like half-cooked noodles when she followed him. She felt like a ghost in a labyrinth of hallways she didn't remember traversing before.

When she stepped outside, that gorgeous and mysterious perfume filled her lungs like an old comfort. She felt drunk on the magnificent scent and knew she never wanted to go back to the blankness of solitary again. But the sky radiated an overpowering bright, electric-blue and the fireball sun sent daggers though her eyes.

Damn the light sensitivity.

She needed the police sunglasses back home on her nightstand. She shaded her eyes with her palm but her pupils were optical lenses with the aperture stuck on nuclear blast.

White, 3D-machine printed buildings now replaced the temporary tents that had been there the night of her arrival. It was like a plastic, hexagonal city without seams had gone up while she was locked down.

Really? The future couldn't still be made out of wood, or even hemp, or an old classic like concrete?

The ground was still just dirt.

The soldier showed her to her new barracks with the red letter H at the entrance. She found her bed with the general population. The nurse drones whirred around, marginally attending to people's needs, dispensing drugs. Trinity talked to some nearby people, but she kept her head down, her eyes averted. She didn't want to be recognized. Everyone was afraid, anyway. Fear and pain ruled.

Mostly they were all in bed, unable to organize or resist or do anything. No one even talked of escape, the idea was too exhausting. When you had Chronic, a lot of what you did was just stare at walls. It's all your brain could do.

Trinity joined them.

Her symptoms got worse.

Weeks passed.

SHE FINALLY FELT LIKE SHE COULD TAKE A LONGER WALK. THE spring air was crisp. The mysterious perfume was only a whiff in the air today, but Trinity closed her eyes and inhaled like she might be healed just from that heavenly scent.

The Western perimeter of the camp was made of twenty-foot tall conical fence posts that radiated a dangerous red laser fence. Black-and-white signs warned of lethal consequence in twelve languages.

In other words, the lasers were not going to give a mild warning stun, they were going to barbecue.

Black tactical drones hovered in strategic positions, monitoring. The peaceful landscape of green fields and hills beyond the barrier faded into a pastel horizon. Maybe farmland, or grazing areas. No homesteads were in sight.

So basically this was nowhere.

Trinity found the mess hall. Almost no one was there because the nurse drones delivered bedside trays. The buffet food squirmed like it might be on a Petri dish under the microscopic lens of a fingerprint-smudged sneeze barrier. The overcooked scrambled eggs smelled like wet hay. She scooped breakfast onto her gun-metal plate and called it a main course of *unknown.*

Trinity carried her tray and sat heavily at a picnic-style table.

"You come in with the new offload?" a bright-green eyed, red-bearded man announced from the distant catty-corner of the rectangular table. He slid on the bench to sit across from Trinity and stuck out his block of a hand. "Nice to meet you."

Trinity felt overwhelmed by the sudden onset of Friendly Human Contact.

She hesitantly presented her fingers for a handshake. His hydraulic-crush knuckles surprised her with gentleness. "I'm Shaughnessy. Don't eat that cold stuff." He nodded at the sad blob on her plate. "I can get you something cooked up fresh. Have you heard yet? They sacked Washington D.C. just ten minutes ago."

"Oh no," Trinity said, worried about the people who lived there. "The real Washington D.C.? Like blew it up?"

"I dunno. The national news said sacked. They showed pictures of *bandana* terrorists with guns all around the White House." He emphasized the word.

They were both silent for a beat.

"You gotta brand the bad guys for the show somehow," Trinity mumbled.

Shaughnessy gave her a sideways look as he examined her face and she worried she'd said too much.

"So what are the latest countries this time?" She didn't worry about sounding uneducated in a concentration camp, but her eyes did dart to the corners of the room where the drones hovered with their supersonic ears. "I mean, I never saw the end of the news broadcast when they had announced the new World War."

"The usual suspects," Shaughnessy answered carefully.

Trinity ran her fingers though her hair. She knew what he meant. War was a racket. How much was propaganda, how much was real, how could you know?

"The Washington D.C. thing will be a distraction," she said. Translation: That will keep the public in fear mode and loyal to their corporate savior.

Shaughnessy seemed to consider her words. He unfolded himself and stood up. Practically an Irish giant. The normal-sized bench table looked like it was a tinker-toy construction that would topple if mistakenly bumped by his muscly thigh. "Like I said, something cooked fresh? Let me show you the ropes around here, skin 'n' bones."

He offered his hand to help her up and Trinity didn't hesitate to feel his gentle touch again.

So many white walls, so many white hallways, so exhausting to walk—but Shaughnessy led her gently. They came to a door which unlocked when he scanned the V2 tattoo on his wrist. A colorful kitchen leapt into view.

Hanging pots and pans gleamed with reflected silver winks and the room exploded with a rainbow of various fruits and vegetables sitting in bins on the wire racks of shelves.

On closer inspection, the produce was blemished or moldy. "Volunteered to cook," he declared proudly, indicating himself with a bow. A few other people shuffled nearby, focused on their cooking tasks. "It's my shift," he added.

"Just make sure to avoid the cabbage."

He looked at her oddly, not getting the reference. Suddenly she noticed the faded Erythema migrans rash on his forearm. "You were bit recently?"

He nodded. "All the luck. Hunting deer and got this tick bite on the weekend. In the doctor's office as a precaution on Monday. Forced outta my home on Tuesday. But I'm not a real Chronic like you. Not yet, at least. I'm taking the drugs preventably."

"They don't always kill *Borellia burgdoferri*. It can shape shift into other forms and hide deep in your tissues because it's a stealth infection, it's bacteria that can *think,*" she said defensively, and then regretted it.

"Well, we can only do what the government recommends," he said lightheartedly. "And we're all getting the best treatment here, right? These medical facilities were created to relieve the pressure off our loved ones while the healthy serve the war effort."

Trinity considered the translation: This is all a crock of shit.

Shaughnessy whipped an Army green apron around his waist. The ties barely could tie, and the apron edged up toward looking more like a baby's bib than a man's stain protector. He got busy chopping vegetables and fired up the gas stove.

He looked like a man who rarely chopped vegetables.

Trinity's legs were turning into soggy noodles again. "I think I'll go lay down."

"You're not *just* a young woman with Chronic disease," he said quietly. He stopped chopping and looked up, his green eyes bore into her like he could be a drone probing for information. "Tell me, if you had one wish for all the Chronics, what would it be?"

Trinity's damaged mitral heart valve started acting up. *Pound, pound, pound.* She didn't know what to say.

"Because you just seem like someone who knows more than she lets on," he continued.

"I don't," Trinity said. "I don't even go to school anymore."

"What would you wish for us?"

"I don't know."

"Well, what have you been doing these years you've been sick?"

"Lying in bed."

"Lying in bed doing what?"

"Staring at walls."

"Staring at walls doing what else?"

"Looking at my cell phone."

"And what was on your phone?"

"The Chronic forums and my websites."

Shaughnessy laughed outright, a happy, jackhammering thud of a laugh that released the pressure of the moment. "I knew it," he said. "You're *the* Trinity. I think we're forum friends."

Trinity could breathe again. That's all he'd been wondering. "Really, we're friends?" She tried to recall all the tiny little photographs in the alternative Chronic treatment groups she frequented online. "What's your name?"

"V.I. Warshawski."

"I thought you were a girl who liked mystery novels?"

"Negatory on the girl part," Shaughnessy confessed. "It's a long story."

"That must take a lot of work, making your fake account seem legit so Universal One doesn't cancel it," Trinity said. "So who is the real Shaughnessy?"

"Sometimes you can't be yourself."

Trinity nodded, her exhaustion canceling her intrigue. "Sounds complicated. I'm just one person and it's hard enough to keep up with my feed. I mean—it was…" Her muscles started in with *twitch, twitch, twitch.*

"But you kept up with it all so well," Shaughnessy said softly. He took Trinity gently by the elbow. She didn't think anything of his kindness at the time.

She leaned on his strong arm the whole way back to her plastic 3D-printed building with an H. She was too fatigued to realize until much later that there was no logical way Shaughnessy would have been part of the Chronic *underground*. Not on the forums. Not anywhere.

Chronic meant untold years of degenerative suffering. Desperation drove you underground, outside and beyond the sham of the recommended pharmaceutical drugs—where patients broke the law to realize they could help each other, help themselves.

And Shaughnessy had *just recently* gotten sick.

TRINITY WOKE SUDDENLY IN THE MIDDLE OF THE NIGHT AS SHE lay underneath her wool blanket in her cot. The ceiling rained those eerie blue service lights down on the lumpy medicated figures in rows. There were groans and smells but Trinity had long ago rigged up a double-tied sock filter that she wrapped around her face each night to breathe.

It worked like a charm.

But she had a creepy feeling now.

She pulled the sock filter slowly off her face and pushed herself up on one elbow to look around the darkened room. What had woken her?

Something yellow flew out from underneath her cot and nudged her arm.

Trinity yelped in surprise.

A nurse drone whirred up to her face, a bobbing white sphere with that big red plus sign. A panel opened and a probe extended with a language sensor. *"Comment allez-vous?"* it said in French.

"Sweet Jesus," a conspiratorial voice whispered from under Trinity's cot. "Make the stupid piece of junk go away."

Trinity's heart just about beat out of her chest. She took a few deep breaths, trying to find her voice.

"Just another nightmare tonight," she explained to the drone. It self-corrected to the English language and dispensed a pill. Trinity accepted the sleeping drug, decided to swallow it, and the drone whirred away having accomplished its job.

"It's just me Shaughnessy," the voice under her bed whispered. "I was just trying to nudge you awake."

"Consider that accomplished." Trinity's mind tried to wrap around the idea that the hulking Irishman could fit underneath her cot. She draped her body upside down and looked at the narrow space between the bed frame and the floor. A baby yellow orb hummed near the ground. Its polished sides were spherical and without identifiers. It had two little green aperture lights as eyes.

"What are you doing, Shaughnessy?" Trinity whispered harshly. "Don't get me back in solitary with this stolen tech. It might be considered a terrorist act in here."

"It's not stolen." Shaughnessy's disembodied whisper sounded hurt. "And it's got superior capabilities, like making V2's malfunction."

Trinity flashed back to her first night in the camp. Her V2 tattoo had malfunctioned then, showing only a single white pixel. But all that didn't matter now. She was in too much pain.

"Fly away before a black Tactical comes in here."

"But you never answered my question about the wish, Trinity."

"Oh good Lord," she said. "Why are you asking me this now? Have you lost your mind?"

"Please, Trinity. If you answer then I'll know for sure. I need to know."

Trinity fell back onto her pillow in exasperation. She pulled the wool covering over her head. The yellow orb nudged her blanket like a little insistent kitten, scrunching up the fabric until it wiggled its way inside. Trinity quickly closed her fingers around the drone and held it in her hand like a golf ball. "I swear I'll smash you against the wall," she whispered to her clenched fist.

Shaughnessy was silent.

"Okay. Fine." Trinity thought for a moment, trying to organize her brain cells to focus on the research she had studied in PubMed, the online database of scientific papers that most of the general public didn't know existed. But she too was exhausted to think through all that stuff. It didn't matter anymore.

None of it mattered.

"I would just wish for all the Chronics to be healed." She closed her eyes.

When Trinity woke up in the morning, the yellow orb was still clutched in her palm. The big white lights overhead signaled daytime in the windowless enclosure and some people were moving about. A spike of dread fanned out through her chest.

"Shaughnessy," she whispered. "Why is your drone still in my hand? Are you still there?"

The orb felt dead inside her fingers.

Exasperated even more than before, Trinity wondered where she should hide it. She opened her fingers and it kicked to life, the two green eyes blinking. She snatched at it but it danced away, making a twittering sound, hovering at the edge of her bed.

Trinity tossed off her blanket and snatched at it again, but the orb had great reflexes. She walked discretely along the row of beds, smiling at a few of her Chronic neighbors but still trying to keep her face hidden, secretly snatching at the bubbly little orb like it was a bratty little brother trying to get her in trouble.

She burst out of the barracks door, the sunlight blinding. Her legs stumbling. If only she had her police sunglasses to cut the springtime glare.

"Stop it," she whispered.

The yellow orb was playing a game.

It wandered along the dirt a few inches above the surface, darting between other people's feet, flirting with danger. Trinity moved as fast as her tired legs would let her, heading toward the Eastern border of the camp.

She'd never wandered over this way before.

The plastic barracks ended with the letter Z and kept going with the letters AA. How big was this place? And no obvious soldiers in fatigues to be seen—though they must be around—just disheveled Chronics with their parchment-paper faces wearing moss-green pants and white T-shirts, shuffling here, shuffling there. Never very far.

White helper drones for the drugs and camp instructions.

Black enforcer drones for solitary.

And not a damn thing else.

She had assumed there were soldiers in fatigues busily running the place. At least a center of command. It dawned on Trinity that bigwigs didn't really need to run the place because Chronics could be pushed over with a feather. What was here for a bigwig to order a soldier to do? Not much. Soldiers were used to drive the transport trucks, but that was it. They were then dispatched elsewhere to fire machine guns for World War Somewhere.

This was a forgotten camp.

A place to offload the Chronic problem, and Chronic voices, until Corporate One could cover up the mismanaged secret that the disease had been unleashed on its own people as a biological weapon.

This kind of tactic went back as far as the Roman Empire. Maybe farther. Keep a percentage of the populace consumed day-to-day with mere survival, and there would be no time for anything else—including organized resistance.

Bio-engineered chemicals, delivered in bacteria, was only one leg of the giant octopus of social control. Corporate One just didn't want the rest of the healthy public to know the dirty truth.

It wasn't good for their brand-spanking-new benevolent image.

It especially wasn't good for taking over the world and getting away with it.

The yellow orb was zooming faster. It burst into a clearing of thin grass and weeds, beyond the last white building with a ZZ tag.

The giant laser fence towered above Trinity's head with a zapping click every few seconds. Trinity's eyes finally focused beyond the fence, into the free zone. An almond orchard stood with majestic trees and vibrant pink blossoms, right out of a fairytale.

The biggest smile grew on Trinity's face.

Like a lightning bolt the yellow orb zipped backwards and tapped Trinity on her V2 tattoo with a soft *doink*. She glanced at the screen. It had that white blinking pixel.

"Shaughnessy," Trinity whispered. "Are you sure it's malfunctioning again?"

The bratty brother winked an eye and shot though the laser boundary unharmed, disappearing into the magical pink wonderland.

Trinity hesitated a moment. Then she ran through the laser fence, and yes—she ran.

THE YELLOW ORB BOBBED ALONGSIDE HER.

The gorgeous fragrance, the incredible canopy of pink-and-white blossoms over a carpet of green grass, the raindrop kiss of delicate petals falling on her skin, the exotic nut-honey taste on the tip of her tongue.

Trinity heard herself giggling out loud.

And oh, the buzzing of happy honeybees. A million busy bees pollinating the flowers, zipping here and there. They were amazing.

In the distance, some kind of classic red Corvette convertible with a bold white stripe sat parked under the canopy of a row of trees. Shaughnessy leaned back against the closed driver door. He might roll the classic car over on its side and crush it if he wasn't careful.

The yellow orb flew into his hand.

Trinity stopped walking.

"The bandanas aren't the bad guys," he called out across the distance. "We aren't ever portrayed fairly, either. We don't even blow things up. Not one thing."

"I know that." The exhaustion in her body doubled up on her. That noodle feeling was growing in her legs. "But what I can't figure out is what you want with me. I'm dying. Don't you get it? We're all dying of this disease. You might too, Shaughnessy. And it will be a miserable end-stage."

"Not if we have a cure."

"Don't say cure. Universal One doesn't want a cure. I thought you *got* that. There will never be a cure allowed. Chronic has a political job. A nefarious job. It's doing its job."

"Trinity, you're a superstar in the Chronic underground. You have thousands of followers in the forums." Shaughnessy pushed off the door and the frame of the car squeaked back and forth on its wheels. "You've documented about every alternative treatment from around the world. Herbs, rife machine, deep nutrition, detox—all the stuff most of the mainstream doctors won't touch. You've helped so many people manage their symptoms. Chronic has a high suicide rate. People who might've taken their lives otherwise, but they found you instead. You're a kind-hearted leader in the Chronic underground, with a health manifesto—patients taking their healing into their own hands and out of the government's."

She couldn't help but laugh. Calling her a *leader* was seriously over the top. Who could *lead* anything from bed?

When Shaughnessy didn't alter his earnest expression, Trinity even rolled her eyes.

He held up a book that had been tucked behind his back. His honest eyes were green pools of light in the sun. "The only treatment you missed is this one. All the copies had been destroyed. This might be the last book that exists. It's the game changer."

Trinity decided to sit on her knees in the soft grass. "What could I have possibly missed?" she said.

He walked toward her. The neurological pains shot down her arms and legs like razor blades. She let him see her cry.

She never, *never* let anyone see her cry. She *never* talked about the unbearable pain.

Shaughnessy wiped a burning tear from her cheek with a cigar finger. "Look," he said. His other hand extended the book toward her like a sacred object. Trinity squinted at the bright cover in the sun and Shaughnessy awkwardly, but kindly, tried to shade her eyes.

The Bee Venom Miracle by Vernon Peabody Atherton, M.D.

It had been published in 1915.

TRINITY FELL ASLEEP IN THE BACKSEAT OF THE CLASSIC CAR. Shaughnessy had lunch wrapped in a basket when she woke. She picked at her zesty ham and mozzarella sandwich. The odd thing was, he might actually be a good cook.

Apitherapy had been practiced by the ancient Egyptians, Chinese, and Greek. Even the founder of modern medicine: Hippocrates. Bee venom may have been the original acupuncture needle. The use of all the bee hive products included: honey, pollen, propolis, royal jelly and bee venom.

You started with stinging the back with a test sting and pulling it immediately to make sure you didn't have an allergic reaction; then to build up tolerance to the treatment. Then you could branch out to treat extremities. Bee venom was known well for treating rheumatics and arthritic joints. Big Pharma had even managed to get bee venom into a modern needle (but of course they weakened the medicine to a moot point).

There was melittin in the venom. It killed infections by poking holes in biofilm. There was more that wasn't fully understood—but people healed.

Mother nature might have a leg up over biotech. An ancient leg. It could work.

It could really work.

"How did you find me? How did I happen to be in the camp by this almond orchard? And at springtime when the bees are here for pollination? How did this all come together?"

Shaughnessy shrugged. "I know tech." He glanced at Trinity's V2 and nodded. "I can find anyone. We knew Chronic was a biowarfare agent and the bandanas have been looking for a cure. But the orchard and the bees? That

I can't explain. Maybe the bad guys don't always win in the end. Maybe sometimes luck gets stacked on the good side, our side."

Shaughnessy handed her a cell phone. "Be gentle with yourself, my heroine."

Trinity reached eagerly for the device, and then a connection to the internet was finally in her hands and she was scared to look.

Her forum profiles were erased. Her websites were down. Her email scrubbed. It was like she had never existed on the web. In the world at all.

"But you're still alive in their hearts," he said. "Loyalty made from gratitude cuts a river deep. Stop hiding and show the people in this camp who you are. They'll follow. We'll give it three months. Then six if we can. Record the data points of each patient, how symptoms improve. What Corporate One has given us is the location to run our own clinical trials in a way we could have never dreamt possible. And all with one of nature's most amazing little creatures."

"Because Rome eventually fell," she whispered. "No matter how many octopus legs it had."

Trinity ignored Shaughnessy's quizzical look—closing her eyes, listening to the bees buzz over their heads. She had to admit it was an unnerving treatment. How painful could it be? Desperate times, desperate measures.

"So are you going to do the honors?"

Shaughnessy gave her a test sting one inch from the spine on her middle back. All she could say after that was a cluster of bad words that had Shaughnessy doubled over laughing like he might bust a gut.

"There's one thing I want to know," she said. "Why did you force me to tell you what I wished for?"

"Because a wish is a form of hope," he said. "And hope makes us want to live, makes us brave."

And she had thought she understood what he meant.

THEY WORKED OUT A SCHEDULE.

Shaughnessy had a hidden stash of hives on the orchard. The queen bees laid over a thousand eggs a day, and the average worker bee lived for six weeks. Shaughnessy collected the elders in their last weeks of life and got them through the laser fence in mason jars, safe from the Three Point Tacticals.

Trinity stung herself on her back with six-inch reverse tweezers and a mirror for two months, alone, because Shaughnessy wasn't in the camp anymore—made note of her fears and the early signs of symptomatic relief, and then set up a secret sting clinic.

She was excited.

No, she was ecstatic.

Her twitching reduced. Her fatigue was better. Everything was going swimmingly. Yes, the stings hurt. It was better than dying.

"The first months are going to be a rollercoaster," she'd explained to the volunteers from barracks H. "There's die-off from the bacterial war inside our bodies. We're gonna have the Herxheimer reaction. That means we will feel worse before we feel better because of the toxins released from dead spirochetes. We have to take care of each other, but at the same time we need to run this camp like we're all still sick. The drones can't know what we're doing. The soldiers that come through here periodically can't know. And we have to stop swallowing their poison drugs."

The sting clinic was in the kitchen. They all read the secret bee venom book and learned the procedure. Everybody chose their sting dose based on their different body reactions. They all had to make their own decisions.

And now, thanks to Shaughessy, Trinity's malfunctioning V2 tattoo had new abilities, like opening every door in the camp. In fact, all the patients in the sting trials had upgraded V2's.

They hid the therapy bees in the mason jars behind the fruits and vegetables, under towels to keep it dark and hive-like, and lovingly fed them raw honey. Patients filtered in throughout "sting day" for stings on their backs, giving each other secret high-fives while new life stirred inside their tired eyes.

It was medicine with a kick. No one complained that it was painful.

Okay, everyone complained.

But they were getting better, to varying degrees, and everyone wanted to continue. They wanted to become beekeepers when they were free again. Three months. Then six. Some thought it could be a cure. Others thought it might only be a palliate, but a great one at that.

And then that fateful day came when the big Army

trucks rolled in like thunder. And the muscly soldiers unloaded their big guns and followed the terrible orders they'd been commanded to follow.

Because in wartime soldiers shoot with machine guns, that's what they're trained to do.

BEGINNING OF WINTER, LATER THAT YEAR—

Dear Shaughnessy,

I never got a chance to say thank you.

After they started burning the camp I ran to save the hives, but they were burning, too. I don't know how I got away. I didn't want to survive at first. I remember walking the fields for days in the hot summer sun. Eating blackberries. Drinking dirty water from the drainage ditch.

Convoys of military tanks and trucks came and went. Somehow they never found me.

I think I know the real reason you made me make a wish that morning. You knew all along what would happen and I didn't. You were trying to protect me, to give me a survival tool, the same one you had.

You were wrong about just one thing.

A wish isn't just a form of hope to use for self-preservation—it can become a life mission to give hope to other people, too. Even when you're not sure you want to live for yourself, you can live for others. You can give hope to others.

I'm in complete remission—maybe that's a cure? I want to give this therapy to humanity.

I wear a bandana now.

I'm not giving up on the Chronics or bee sting therapy. I look forward to our meeting in January because we can still save the world from this tyranny.

Warmly,
Trinity Jane (The Sting Girl)

THE DISINVENTION OF THE SURVEILLANCE STATE

MACAPA, *Brazil*
1994

THE JUNGLE NEVER GETS AMNESIA.

Never forgets it has a soul.

It has a memory all the way back to when it first grew primordial and the animals left enormous footprints. It hums with that ancient shit, and when you walk like a city slicker with your little factory Vibram soles and anti-dandruff shampoo in a plastic pop-top in your backpack, right into the jungle's waiting emerald embrace; you don't know what you've done.

The jungle gets its hooks in you.

That's why it *has* hooks, so they can get in you.

You don't know the jungle is eating into you a little more every day, changing you. Everything is sneaking in under your skin. It stings, bites, or sticks to you so much you stop swiping at it. Crawls up under your pant legs, gets into your lungs, fills you up everywhere until you know you're suffocating in the green—every visible color of green and even more green you can't see. And you'll never wash your skin enough to get the touch of it off.

Not ever again.

Because you'd have to scrub your skin to the bone.

So instead, you just say: I am not myself anymore.

When you admit that, the jungle has won, and it will now leave you alone.

But I didn't know all that when I stood on a rickety, wooden dock over the gunky brown Amazon river and thought about corporate piranha in business suits. I was fifty-seven years old.

A Catholic nun; not really, but I was dressed like one. All black-and-white.

Mikhal Costa found me easy, loose-jointed and lively, brown-eyed—he didn't walk, he jaunted. Happy young fellow; I'd go so far as to say wise.

He had something I didn't have. I wasn't jealous. Happiness amused me.

He was one-quarter each French, Spanish (father's side), Portuguese, and Canadian First Nation (mother's side). That didn't explain why he had a Russian first name. He became my friend because he knew I'm American, and paid him good money for a jungle tour.

Also, because I had black skin and soft blue eyes.

That goes a long way with people, all over the world. Like two enemies got together and made peace.

I don't know why they assume the peace. Maybe it's

because I'm a wrinkled lady who looks like she's travelled the world but came home to start a roadside shop with an honest dirt floor. I say less than expected, and that has the effect of making people think I've really said more.

Or maybe it's because I have such a nice white toothy smile. And I was compassionate, that can be said, and it's true. I'd played a Red Cross nurse many times, that's useful. That's a foreigner in South America for you.

The air smelled like rancid butter.

My nun's habit was salty hot with the articles I had taped to my body to hide. Sweat kept dripping down my neck like the very fine edge of a knife.

I remember the first step I took into the cargo boat—the chipped, green-pea-soup colored paint on the scarred wood. A splinter stabbed up into my fingernail.

That soup color reminded me of my aunt's shed, where the gardener's kept the nicest gardening tools, back in the 1950s.

My aunt worked for Eisenhower, *under* the gardens. (She even knew him.)

She'd take me inside that shed, privately open a revolving wall with a numeric code. My mouth always got sweaty, when the blue lights came on, and I saw the iron spiral stairs.

My Lucille Ball's clanked on the rungs. And that filtered air came up; came up dense and cold.

I hated the skirts we had to wear.

I wore boy's trunks underneath, because us girls learned to kick fight on the wrestler's mats down there, under the bare bulbs that were angry as the sun. And if I caught half my aunt's black South African face in the wrong glare of those brilliant lights: She looked split, one-side white.

Isn't that how it goes.

That's how my uneasy history came back to me. My first day on the Amazon river and the jungle's already got a way to make me reflect.

The slate-blue clouds cast shadows on the water's surface, between bulky cargo boats carrying bananas, pigs, furniture, rice—because the river *is* the road—and the shadows rippled, undulated, like unnatural black ink. All kinds of ghosts or snakes. Or bad shamanic visions. And I knew if I leaned over too far, I would see my blue eyes looking back up at me.

So I didn't lean over.

Some things you get tired of seeing.

Mikhal Costa and I lay in the lower deck in orange hammocks that night, near the toilets. The silver moon came out. You could see the soft blue glow of people with smartphones. The water slapped the boat's wooden planks like flatulence. Samba played out of a cassette tape machine. Antarctica Cerveja bottles clanked upstairs where a lively game of Truco was being played.

That was when the mosquito drone bit me.

I had slapped my neck on impulse, just thinking it was a regular jungle bug. Drove the micro needle in deeper.

Unobtrusive, pervasive, lethal.

The payload could be anything. Could be nanobots, RFID. Virus. I examined the crushed technology in my palm.

Hello, enemy. How shall we war, today?

That's how it is. You try to outplay the other player until they outplay you.

I'd just been outplayed.

I waited for a reaction. None. Localized itching. Probably tracking bots, then.

I have to hand it to the Catholic nuns, though; these obnoxious black-and-white garments could hide a satellite. I had my own tech with me. I even had multiple stashes of my own sanitary wipes in Ziplocs. Sometimes, when you need to befriend a tourist, clean white toilet paper is the ticket. Valued more than pure gold in the correct moment.

But my G4 drone kit I wore under my armpit was gone.

Gone.

And I'd just been injected with it.

I ate my breakfast out of a KitKat wrapper saved from the airport in Narita—(and if this is your first time savoring a green Japanese KitKat, we'll have to get weird and wacky) —and sucked the white stuff off some Inga pods, spitting the seeds into the river. I will always think these huge green peas look like mutated caterpillars from the land of Oz.

But they are sweet and smooth, and taste like vanilla ice cream.

The tremendous winding Amazon—a dark, mysterious artery for the blood of planet Earth. It carries more water to the ocean than the Mississippi, the Nile, and Euphrates rivers combined, and it finally spit me out like junk in a remote village, days later, where Mikhal and I disembarked.

My feet were swollen.

I watched the pink dolphins jump.

Women in Western clothing washed laundry in a stream. Huts with thatched roofs sat squat, children playing *futebol,* lazy smoke drifting into the sky as it turned red and purple.

We put our gear into a small canoe with an outboard motor that spit blue sparks and hissed like a snake. I coughed on pungent diesel fumes. Mikhal got supplies, and a big box of fish on ice to be delivered upstream.

The tributary, Rio Jaracu, narrowed like a trachea being crushed.

Mikhal and I spoke like old friends. The Amazon does that.

The light was blue-black twilight, with the canopy overhead, then there's a Macaw in bright scarlet, yellow, and blue. I think those parrots are out of place. Inner city graffiti in spray paint. But they have tails like flashing Samurai swords, and beaks sharp as the blade on my steel karambit.

And they can scream, too.

The whole jungle is as dense as a super-big head of broccoli. And this part of the jungle smells like every fresh vegetable on earth spun up in a blender and made into juice, plus a splash of flower fragrance, too.

You breathe it in; and it never quite breathes out all the way.

Mikhal says we need to watch for the narcos at night.

I looked out for the narcos. They're using Russian

remote minisubs here to haul cocaine now. But they're not my beat.

I'm here for the soybeans.

American soybeans in Brazil.

It's not that there is no value assigned to the jungle. It's that the value is too high. When you want to control the enemy, you have to control the wild places.

So it's not *really* about soybeans in Brazil.

It's about anything, the best thing, to get in there and get the job done. Make things in your image so you can admire your reflection—the surveillance state.

Encourage this: Clear and burn the land.

We were looking for a manageable percentage.

Make Brazil into the number one exporter of soybeans with a crop in need of acid-neutralizing lime, pesticides, herbicides, fertilizers. Harvesting with John Deere combines, pouring rivers of golden soy into open-bed trucks.

The polished new silos.

No worries about the stolen land.

The locals, they called them *grilagem,* from the Portuguese word *grilo,* or cricket. For how the illegal land grabbers would age a phony land title in a box full of hungry crickets.

I didn't question my assignments. You're not trained to question your assignments. If they think you are questioning your assignments—

I'm a patriot. I won't lie. I had a career, I had a pension.

I wasn't trying to do wrong, I was trying to do right. I

wanted my country to be the one with a leg up. Don't we all?

Did I think about who had stolen my drone and deployed it against me? Yes, I did. The enemy is always near. But fear didn't stop me.

That's the story I told myself, at least. But the jungle had another story to tell this old woman.

Late that night our motorized canoe washed up on a muddy bank. I put on my kindly, wise missionary face in the dark so it would be there when the dawn came.

I'm so not religious.

I wasn't even spiritual, then.

I admit I was annoyed to be playing the enduring metaphor for the colonial destruction of tribal peoples. But after I secured my hidden tech, I was getting rid of the full habit.

It was too damn hot to wear.

What I didn't know is how easily these tribal people had already outsmarted me.

In retrospect, I knew the pre-Columbian peoples had created highly developed civilizations. I'd been taught they'd all been vanquished. What I didn't think about were descendants.

Having their own secrets.

And that they had been on vigilant lookout for lost souls just like me.

I WAS GIVEN THE PREVIOUS CHRISTIAN MISSIONARY'S accommodations—a square thatched hut, graciously shared with galloping spiders, opera-singing frogs, and glowing yellow beetles with pitchfork purple fangs.

In the deep jungle, the thatched roof is the TV.

But you lay down and watch it out of fear.

I'm not even going to talk about snakes.

You can point a loaded gun at my face and I can disarm you. Go ahead. But keep me the hell away from snakes. You are going about your business, and then to your horror, there's a snake face right there a few feet from you, and it's been quietly there ready to fang you, for awhile. Snakes are everywhere in the jungle, and honestly, a constant test of the strength of your ability to not pee down your leg.

Carry a machete.

In the morning, on my first day of arrival, I was served cassava chips and smoked fish by a toothy boy. His eyes were a peaceful green. The tribe welcomed me with the smiles and the faces that only a spiritual healthy people possess.

I didn't wear that face.

I kept thinking: These are unlike the people I expected to meet. To befriend. To betray. On the second day, the *xama* requested to see me.

Mikhal brought me up the side of a mountain on a narrow jungle trail. Just when we reached the shaman's hut, thunder crashed and the sky broke open. We were engulfed in a roar of warm water, a million droplets dancing in instant mud puddles.

Mikhal shouted over the noise that he needed to head back to Macapa, to his family. When I needed to return, I could send word.

I had generously overpaid him.

We hugged goodbye.

The shaman sat alone on a rug in the middle of the plain hut made of wooden poles. He wore a solid white tunic, and an orange feathered hat over his bowl cut hair. His salt-and-pepper mustache complemented his salt-and-pepper beard. Colorful beaded necklaces adorned his neck. His very dark eyes sparkled with light. He called to me in English, waved me over like he was keeping the seats for a Knicks game and I was holding the Coke and hot dogs.

"Come over, come over." I almost thought I detected a New York accent. "I'm Hernan de Cortez."

My jaw slackened in a little bit of surprise.

I almost said, like the conquistador who—

But I nodded okay, instead. Sometimes, either people are playing with you, or there's an irony to the world, and you don't have to mention it.

Hernan winked at me with those sparkling eyes, anyway, and I sat on the mat in front of him. I sat cross-legged like a westerner, my knees jacked up like mountain peaks to rest my elbows.

There was smoke in the air; it smelled like cinnamon.

He was older than me, in a limber body a quarter his age. He sat relaxed like a yoga master.

"I have something to return to you." The wrinkles around his eyes danced. "I apologize for any inconvenience."

I wasn't playing dumb. I really thought it was going to be a jungle shaman thing, even if he'd been educated, you know what I mean? A wood carving. A little woven basket. Some nice herbs.

He pulled my G4 drone kit out of his white tunic. It's a ballistic rectangular black box. Waterproof, shock proof. It has a biometric lock and only opens to my fingerprint.

It was open.

Mosquito drone gone.

My enhanced smart phone lay there with its colorful screen alive with a contour map in 3D geography. A blue dot blinked. He extended it out to me on his open palm. "You are welcome in the jungle, under our care, for as long as it takes to find yourself here."

For the second time, I felt my jaw slacken.

I surmised the blue dot was me.

My hand wanted to flutter to the area of the fake mosquito bite on my neck. Like I could block the RFID signal.

But I'm trained to not give that kind of tell.

Finally, I took the black box softly from his hands. My brain was clicking into gear. Howler monkeys calling in the distance sounded like monsters—terrifying, deep, grunting.

I realized the rain had stopped. Now the jungle held its breath.

"I believe I find myself on unsure footing," I finally said.

"Going up the mountain, or coming down?"

I didn't understand the question. I looked him in the

eye. I sensed no hostility. Indeed, I perceived a kindness that unnerved me. An educated intellect that outmatched mine.

"May I ask how you acquired this?"

"I believe I found it under your left armpit."

That seemed true enough. My next question was, how? I scanned through all the faces from the boat I could remember. I had not met Hernan before. Ever.

Hernan just smiled a beautiful, toothy smile.

His spy craft was better than mine.

I set the drone paraphernalia between us, like I didn't need to take it back. He could have it. But my spy craft guts were pretty much spilled at this point. I had my karambit secretly strapped to my thigh. The blade felt hot, like it was branding me.

He must have sensed my unease.

No doubt he had his own hidden weapons, right?

"Please, my friend, you will find no enemies here." Hernan unfolded his legs and stood in one fluid motion. "Let me show you, will you come?"

I stood up as well, but much more arthritically.

I followed him behind the hut and down a narrow path. Bright blue morpho butterflies fluttered past. Giant leaves tickled my bare arms. I felt the jungle plants slowly moving in, tightening, like the vines were going to lash around my ankles and wrists and pull me to the ground.

Eat me.

My mouth got sweaty.

Hernan led the way. But I felt like he was watching me

somehow out of the back of his orange feather hat. Or that the jungle had hidden eyes, and they were judging me.

I heard the pounding roar of the waterfall before I saw it; gorgeous blue pouring liquid and just then the sun broke out and turned the falls into sparkling white crystals. A slippery, rocky path we tread, and then into a dim musky cave behind the falls.

"Just a moment of pitch darkness coming," Hernan said. "Please keep your hand to the wall."

Cool air brushed my face.

I dragged my fingers against the smooth stone and found a groove, a channel. It must have been worn there by a million other fingers, dragging. The ancestors.

The pre-Colombian ones.

Jealousy needled me. I wanted to have *this* kind of history, this kind of deep definition. Instead, I had never even known my real parents. And after my aunt was murdered, so was any South African connection.

I had belonged to the State since I was seven.

Then all the light died. It was an abyss. I could hear only Hernan's footsteps padding in front of me. He told me to turn left and ascend the stone steps, don't slip. The jealousy in me scurried away like a rat.

Now, I felt fear.

Waves of it crashing over me, pummeling me. Were it not for the finger groove, I think I would have screamed.

Then *bam*, we were in a vast cavern filled with the softest, most peaceful light.

To this day, I cannot fully describe what I saw. Not in its full glory. Not in the way it struck me.

I saw a giant cavern filled with magnificent ancient cave paintings. Images covered every surface, from walls to ceiling. The floor was stone so polished it winked like wax. And these were not crude hand prints—these ancient works of art rivaled Michelangelo, Rembrandt.

No, they surpassed.

I realized I was in a chapel, or a temple. Someplace that had been sacred, that still *was.*

In the center of the room a stone circle rose, just like a meditation cushion.

But the light? What made the room so filled with light? We were a hundred miles from electricity, from gas.

There were no flickering fire torches on the walls.

Hernan touched my shoulder. I felt like I'd waited a hundred years to feel his touch. I couldn't pull my eyes away from the paintings.

"If they had their own technologies, in the world before now, why do we assume it would mirror our own?" Hernan spoke so softly, I could barely hear his voice. "Or would it be mysterious, unrecognizable—or even invisible to untrained eyes?"

I understood.

The room made me understand.

All your questions will be answered here.

I sat back to back with Hernan on the stone meditation circle. Our knobby spines interlocked like a jigsaw puzzle. He gave me my first lesson in shamanism.

I cried.

Stay in the jungle, come back to the temple until you know what you need to know.

Months passed on the banks of the Amazon, and they were the most amazing, adventurous years of my life. I felt like a young Indiana Jane with the tribe—no, I felt like a real human being.

I felt honest for the first time in my life.

In one of our sessions, Hernan used the word Globalists: They are the power elite you have spied for. They have infiltrated every country. They wish to bring about a one world order, ruled by evil. They have no particular race, creed, or culture—they are the souls who have chosen darkness.

They are unwell.

They pray to demons.

And the time comes, we must rise up and take back the Earth from them, and destroy the infrastructure they have built to enslave us.

There is a great battle between light and dark, going on for thousands of years. We are coming to the darkest time, just before the dawn.

Just before light wins.

I memorized Hernan's words.

And then one day, I found my own face on the ancient cave wall.

My blue eyes, black skin, the curve of my cheekbones. My mosquito drone. There were many other faces beside me—some I knew, some I figured I had yet to meet.

The Globalists had used me to build their Empire. And planned to enslave us all inside it.

I don't know how I could have been so stupid.

It was time to untwiddle my thumbs and change my attitude. It was time to stop working for *them.*

I had to leave the Amazon.

I won't let their Empire be the world I leave for you.

THE RESISTANCE HEADQUARTERS

Anywhere, Everywhere

LAST WEEK IN THE LABORATORY, I WAS FINALLY INJECTED WITH a successful serum of *Pestalotiopsis microspora.* That's a fungus that eats plastic, like seek-and-destroy. I'm in awe of it. The jungle has given us the antidote for nanotechnology, it ate the RFID in my bloodstream.

Globalists: This is what we're all telling you.

Be afraid.

Because we're the elite operatives you trained, who have turned on you, and you don't know what countries we come from, or how we organize, or what technologies we have access to put to positive, healing use.

Positive, without exception.

We work for the Earth now. Good people, animals, plants, land, water, insects, air. Why not the stars, too.

Everything we did for evil, we will undo.

THE MONSTER EXPERIMENT

I DIDN'T PARK my little dark green Toyota truck in front of his house. It seemed too obvious. I had called ahead, sure. He knew I was coming, sure.

But my truck and his house, they were two things that just didn't go together.

So I parked a few blocks away on a side street in front of a quaintly dilapidated home in a quiet row of other quaintly dilapidated homes. The weeds in the yard were blooming, soft purple little flowers, spilling onto the sleepy sidewalk.

I couldn't really see any people.

Then a few cars drove past on the main street ahead of me. I eyed the indistinct figures of the drivers and no one turned their head to look my way.

I sat holding the steering wheel, feeling like a mutated bacteria strain under a microscope. I hadn't been here in over ten years and I felt squirmy. I kept reminding myself that I didn't *really* see anyone nearby. This was a sleepy

Northern California coastal town. It had one main road. It had one school. One volunteer fire department. It had a few million dollar homes with million dollar views.

But I had one thing narrowed into focus. His sunflower yellow house on the corner lot.

And if anybody recognized me, they weren't going to do anything about it, not right now.

Those purple weedy flowers were peeking up through the cracks in the sidewalk and I mashed one to a pulp under my sneaker as I got out and shut my truck door. It didn't shut it enough. I had to reopen it and shut it again.

Across the intersection ahead of me, about a hundred and fifty feet forward, his front yard was cared for. I didn't know what bothered me. That it was cared for, or that I was so close to it.

He'd put in a little stone patio and some redwood planter boxes with spring flowers. The patio wrapped around the front porch in a little half-crescent extending along the public side of the house. There was that same green bushy tree I remembered that broke out in those red pimple berries. A waxy telephone pole that your eyes ignored. A concrete walkway up to the front door that was trying to look welcoming to strangers. A weathered wooden sign on two sturdy legs was plunged into the ground and announced *Abergren Art.*

Art. Whatever.

I mean, what's the definition of art? Just because you can hold up a brush?

The breeze coming up off the Pacific ocean smelled both fresh and invigorating and a bit like a big salty armpit. I'm not a fish eater. Or those other kinds of seafoods that come in shells. No amount of fancy sauce fixes the bad taste in my mouth.

I didn't feel like a bacterium in a petri dish anymore. I felt like a thirty-two-year-old woman with hips too curvy and legs too long. I reached up and wound my curly hair into a controlled ponytail. I walked the first fifty feet down the sidewalk, the happy-go-lucky sun warming my face and winter-pale arms, and wished I'd dressed in bulky layers like long sleeves and a baggy sweatshirt and a tight jog bra underneath to flatten my assets down—not this stupid shapely cotton V-neck and stylish modern jeans.

I shouldn't have shown this much damn skin.

Those bad feelings were crawling all over me like a skin infection.

Like I could have just started scratching myself all over until my own fingers drew blood and the layers of exposed skin scraped and bunched up under my chewed nails. Because there's always room for something painful to get under your nails, no matter how close to the nub you keep them.

Thirty-five feet.

I could just go ahead and skin myself. Bloody orbs as eyeballs. Show up at his doorstep without a human face and knock.

Hi Dad. It's been a long time. How you doing?

I jogged across the main street. No more traffic. The ocean leapt into view on my left, breathlessly calm and flat as a pancake. Puffy white clouds sailed overhead.

It was beautiful here. That bothered me. This quiet

fishing town with the pier and the little picturesque fishing fleet and surround by the magnificent redwood forests and for fucks sake they'd even filmed some Hollywood blockbusters up here. And everyone had to drive by *Abergreen Art* and that stupid welcoming sign.

And some people even voluntarily went in to his gallery. How crazy was that?

Now I'd just walked up the three concrete steps to his door and I had to lift my whole arm to get my fisted hand to rap on the yellow door. My knuckles made a boneless sound.

I waited. A soft breeze ran over the hair on my arms.

A car finally drove by again, tip-toeing forward like the driver probably eased off the gas from admiring the stunning ocean view. It was two o'clock in the afternoon of a dead Wednesday.

There was a dirty smudge just above his copper doorknob, and another brownish smudge at about chest height right along the door edge. He lived alone here, so it was probably oil from his hands touching that same place over and over.

I didn't want to touch there.

My hearing was on high alert. An American robin (*Turdus migratorius*—and because I'm a bird lover, I know it's the most abundant bird in North America) skittered along the roof gutter, dry bird nails scratching the metal pipe. Far away a child laughed and I felt worried, worried that child didn't know who was behind this painted yellow door, worried that child might wander too close to this house by accident, might even feel like that stupid welcoming sign was *welcoming*, might stand within reach of my father and his long arms.

I heard the floor boards in the house groan. Time slowed, his footsteps behind the closed door slowed, I felt my heartbeat echoing in my chest. I thought I could run fast back to my truck, but I'd be stuck in one of those nightmares where I'm trying to run away from him but time is so slow I can't make any progress. My time gets measured in elongated microseconds and everyone else is faster.

The door swung open and my dad said, "Why hello."

He was definitely shorter, more slouched. The first thing I thought was it's really true you do shrink when you get older.

The man I had remembered was tall. Unnaturally tall.

Or maybe he was just unnatural.

I still had to look up into his dark brown eyes. There's the brown color that's dark, and then there's a darkness behind the color. There are few people in this world that I encounter that I have to look up to, since I'm six two, (you'll never catch me in heels)—but my father is taller than everyone.

I don't like looking up. It forces me to lift my chin. If you've ever seen a hand shoot out of nowhere toward your face, you understand about wanting to keep your chin tucked.

Time gets measured in microseconds.

"Hi, Dad." My gentle voice came out of a throat squeezing closed.

He stepped backward one step. "Well, come on in," he

welcomed. He patted his stomach. He'd always had that awkward behavior. The stomach pat.

I kept looking up into his eyes. I didn't want to see his face. Of course I saw his face—I just mean I didn't want to think about the details.

The smell of his house hit me. Washed up my nose and into my throat. A little bit like old historical newspaper clippings, stewed tomatoes and beans, and a sour undercurrent of male urine. Just an undercurrent.

My senses were sharp.

Maybe my memories were more sharp.

He took a few more steps backward. I moved forward, across the threshold, moving on autopilot, moving on sheer willpower. Then I realized I'd have to shut the door. I touched the knob and pushed it closed and didn't think about hand oils.

I stood in his house.

It was totally different and totally the same. I stood in his sunroom, filled with gray filing cabinets and several desks and some green potted plants and his huge drafting table that was a kindhearted gift for him from my mom in the 1970s just after I was born. She wanted to support his art. I think they were in love once. Way before the divorce. Way before I was fifteen and he moved out and moved here.

Schizophrenic pieces of my childhood were laying all around. Oh God, up on the windowsill sat that playdough-clay face thing I'd made that was glued to a tube sock. Was that in first grade? *Shit.* The marble jar with Grandma's old marbles that used to sit in the farmhouse. A black-and-white photo of my grandparents.

My dad was in the next room now, standing by the wood stove with the flames dancing behind the soot-stained viewing window.

My ears were ringing.

I didn't have my knife in my pocket. I made sure not to bring a weapon.

I just had my truck keys. I reached into my pocket and stuck the thick ignition key between my fingers and made a fist. It's a crude knife that way. My dad didn't notice what I was doing with my hand. He was talking and gesturing and friendly.

My dad wasn't *smart* enough to notice what I was doing with my hand.

That was one thing I'd always known. He had been brute strong. I was smarter. That defined us. And looking at his aging, stooped shoulders, I didn't think he was stronger anymore.

I stepped through the next threshold into the next room, getting deeper into it. Deeper into trouble. His refrigerator sat backed against the wall next to the shut bathroom door. A rundown tiled kitchen counter with dirty stained grout. A dripping faucet, sink stained rust-colored where the drips had splashed over and over. Kitchen cupboards hanging skewed just a bit, the cream-colored paint fingerprint smudged around the knobs. It was like he didn't have money for his small house, but he *did* have money.

Everything here was a choice.

Both my dad and I were making choices.

I tried to let go of the make-shift weapon between my fingers but they were soldered around my keys like a robotic arm. I realized that a hefty swing with his cast iron frying pan would do the job. Or that sharp letter opener jabbed in with a collection of pens in a mason jar.

The single recliner next to the wood-stove had a dusty, circular maple-wood base and what used to be a vibrant, disco-orange 70s cushion. I'd pinched my hands under that chair as a kid. I'd hid scared in the dark behind that chair. My brother one time poured a whole glass of milk over my head while I sat in that chair.

Now it looked like it belonged beside the weekly garbage bins for pickup.

The stained cushion had a butt-indention which sank so far down it was a little obscene, and the chair itself was stuck in an awkward backward position, like it would try to receive you, but you were gambling every time you sank your bones down that the whole thing wasn't going to splinter into pieces.

I was shocked about the condition of that chair.

My dad used to read the Sunday paper in that proud chair when I was a kid. The local paper where the pedophiles put their secret ads for kids in the classified section. I didn't know that big word back then.

I started chewing my lip. There was a piece of skin bothering me, and I wanted to pull it back with my teeth.

My dad was still talking and being friendly and he led me into the next room, which was his little local art gallery. His long arms were gesturing. There were paintings on the many walls, landscapes and some abstracts. Sunlight streaming through the divided windowpanes. I caught a rainbow as the light twisted through the thick glass. And one piece of furniture, like a podium, with a guest book for guests to scribble in.

We walked in a circle through three rooms. I always stayed behind him, watching his body language. And we came back to the start.

I tallied up one closed closet with a doorknob and another wall that I was certain had a secret panel and a cavity behind it. Because—well, ten years ago there had been a closet there, too.

That was it. The tour of his whole small house. And we were standing back by the warm wood stove. My dad offered me homemade chili to eat. I politely declined.

I needed to use the restroom.

I wasn't going to relieve myself in his house. I wasn't going to open the bathroom door and have that male urine smell get stronger, I wasn't going to sit on the porcelain where his skin left oils, I wasn't going unfist my weapon to unbuckle the belt looped around my jeans, or remember any more of anything.

"I have to go," I said.

My dad stood there. He didn't step forward. He nodded. I looked into his eyes but I still couldn't take in his face.

"I might come up in a few days. That okay?"

"That would be great," he said.

I stepped sideways toward the first exit threshold and into his sunroom because I wouldn't let him stand where I couldn't see him. "Have a good afternoon," I called halfway over my shoulder even as I was still eyeing his profile.

"I'm really glad you came over," he said. And I don't know why it bothered me that he sounded sincere.

I opened the door to escape into the fresh ocean air. I tried to touch the doorknob in the same place I'd touched it before—impossible, I know. It occurred to me how thin the line of sanity can be, and that I had to be careful about that line.

You can be the snake charmer in life, or you can be the one who gets bit. Because in this whole game-of-life thing, there's always going to be a snake.

I forced myself to walk, not *run,* back to my truck. It felt like there were a million eyes on my back but there was no one watching.

I SPENT THE NEXT THREE DAYS IN A MOTEL IN THE NEXT TOWN over, working on the novel in a marathon run. I sat holed up at a knee-bonking, cramped desk with my bright laptop screen, drab brown curtains drawn into a permanent indoor nighttime, heater cranked up to tropical, typing furiously about mantis aliens and the end of the world.

The aroma of the empty take-out boxes collecting on the kitchen counter created a new fusion of food funk.

My editor tried to reach me on my cell and I ignored her. My husband Mac called and I didn't ignore him. I had two weeks to deadline. Plenty of time to finish the book.

But it might not be enough time to complete my monster experiment.

I had lied to everyone about what city I was holed up in for the next two weeks to write. A six hundred and fifty-two mile lie to be exact—or the distance between Los Angeles and NorCal. That's either a benefit, or a danger, of the modern cell phone and its singular area code.

When I drove the thirty minutes to my dad's town of Abergren for the second time, I parked my Toyota truck in the same spot, away from his house. This time I dressed in long-sleeve layers and my outfit matched the sky—drab-gray billowing sweatshirt and slate-blue jeans.

It was a cold and secretive Sunday without the sun. There were more people walking about, but I was pretty sure no one noticed me. I was looking for a man's head to turn, for a woman's too-long stare. I was looking for a tell.

But my enemies were either eyeing me from a hidden location or they weren't eyeing me at all.

I knocked on his door then shoved my hands in my pockets and felt the comforting serrated edge of my metal truck key in my pocket.

I forced myself not to make a fist. No weapons here.

My dad opened the door and we repeated the whole charade from the first round.

I knew what to expect so it was easier to walk into his house. I stood with my back to his warm little wood stove, and he handed me a historical printout and talked about some local news. He was on the volunteer fire department. He liked to play tennis. He'd sold his old car and walked to get groceries now. Nothing he said was important, but I listened to every word. Between every word.

I didn't know how to tell him what I came here to say.

My teeth felt glued together like I had lockjaw. I could open my mouth just enough to fire off easy responses and ask simple little questions, but then the tension got strong enough that my teeth just wanted to snap back together.

Keep me silent. Or keep me safe, I wasn't sure.

Then my dad suggested we go for a walk to the beach. I didn't want to be seen with him, not so publicly, but I felt my head nodding yes and my voice saying okay.

The only cool thing about a sniper's head shot is that you'll never feel it. And I thought about that paranoia thing, and the thin line, and the problem with what I was doing in Abergren was that my little monster experiment scared me.

My dad put on a dark blue raincoat and I followed him out the door. The fresh ocean air cleared my lungs of the smell of him. I walked by his side but my eyes always had him in the periphery. I stayed to his right so my own right arm would have an extra second.

There's just some things you learn on your own, and you learn them well.

But there wasn't a single body movement or comment he made that threatened me. He was being humble, in his awkward stomach-patting way. He was *allowing* me to continue visiting him because he was keeping his dark, evil parts deep inside.

He was protecting me from himself. He was genuinely glad to see me. That told me a lot.

His parents were long dead. His wife long gone. He had no siblings. He had a mishmash of quirky friends, I supposed, who didn't know jack-shit about the real man no matter what they thought. He'd had a stroke last month. The kind of loneliness I sensed from him was so vast and empty you could have filled it with a universe and still have room.

I can tell you this—no child ever raises their hand in school and says, I want to be a molester or a murderer when I grow up.

At least, I believe they don't.

My dad and I walked down the main road, white seagulls swooping, the cliff on one side sloping down into the little circular bay and the steel-blue ocean beyond. The little parking lot by the beach led to the little wharf and a fishy restaurant with a view. People were milling around and I think I cared less and less about who was hiding among them.

Dad brought me here to this beach often when I was a kid, and he was the bad man and I was the little girl. That was consuming my mind.

Now I had returned.

It was ten years after the lawsuit I'd filed. Ten years after he paid a lot of money for a defense and my lawyer went pro bono. Ten years after nothing was proved officially one way or the other, except that I made a stand and he admitted nothing.

Except that I was a strong woman and he was still a bad man.

My dad stepped between a rusting VW bus and a sleek

black BMW. I walked around another way and followed him down to the beach. The sand sucked at my shoes. The compact waves curled up and spit themselves onto the shore with a slap and a hiss.

"I'm going to say what I need to say." Finally, the real words inside me were turning into sound. "Can you agree not to respond until I'm done?"

My dad said okay.

I reminded him that he molested me long ago and I wasn't walking beside him right now pretending that he didn't. I told him about the nightmares. I had filed that lawsuit to stand my ground, but that didn't make us equals now. And I said that he was still my dad, and I would respect him as a human being in all ways but if at any moment he threatened me I would defend myself and he would never see me again.

My dad said okay. He just said it like that, *okay*.

That was good enough for me.

We walked toward a big gray rock buried halfway in the sand. The slate sky hung low. He climbed up and sat facing the calm sea. A breeze rumpled his rain hood and I realized I was looking hard at his weathered face. I swallowed the sourness in my throat. A little wash of fear. The extra darkness behind his dark brown eyes had also seeped into the lines of his face, a spiritual shadow. A spiritual ink stain.

I have his broad nose, I have his full lips. Most of all I have his palms and the same knobby knuckles and the middle finger that curves like a bow.

I don't want to be anything related to my father but I look just like him.

I told him about the underground laboratories, the mind-controlled children, the doctors in white lab coats and the hideous tortures that split minds. It makes us dissociative. I told him I knew he was hurt as a child, and I witnessed him being hurt as an adult by powerful people in the criminal organization he belonged to. I said it like that, *criminal organization.*

If no one in his life had ever said they were sorry for his suffering and the way he was raised—I wanted him to know I was sorry for his pain. He must have felt there was no escape. I told him I saw a world with all the odds stacked against the children, and I didn't make excuses for his choices, but I understood why.

It cost me nothing to be kind.

I watched my dad's body language, the hunch of his shoulders. The squeeze of his haunted eyes. It wasn't my job to judge him. Lest I be judged.

And I'm no angel in this world.

I told him I was married now and I was a novelist. I had a good life, a lot of therapy. And I was trying to figure out healing and forgiveness and how humanity can get out of the mess we're in with the cycles of violence.

Then I said it. "I forgive you." All those months practicing that sentence in the mirror. "I forgive you and I love you."

His fingers grasped at the air and held nothing.

I thought about holding his hand for a second, holding

the hand that mirrored my own. Then the cold, fresh air blew across my face and I didn't reach out.

I remembered how I used to think about all the bad people in my childhood. I remembered that I used to think —if we don't kill them, who will? And that's why I don't own a gun. I might use it. I don't want to answer my own question that way.

"Amanda, you need to write your book, and it needs to not be fictional." My dad spoke my name and that startled me somehow—more than what he'd suddenly said. He continued, "You have to write your book even if it's hard on me."

I looked up at my dad's face, but his eyes were glossy and they were fixed on the ocean. We were silent then for a long, deep time.

Then I did reach out and squeeze his hand. It was warmer than mine. Very smooth and soft and I thought about the grandchild he would never know he had.

We just held hands, my monster and I. If the experiment was compassion it didn't cost me anything.

When we moved off the rock the conversation went back to normal, safe little things. And the truth was, I knew we would never speak of the abuse again. It was too hard.

I DROVE BACK TO MY MOTEL ROOM WITH THE TRUCK WINDOWS down and the wind dancing through the cab and my hair blowing around like a party. I felt happy. I'd done the *brave thing*. My monster experiment was working so far.

Back at the motel, I slid my room card into the lock and it clicked. The little light changed from red to green. I pushed the door open to greet my dark writing cave and stepped forward, fingers sliding against the wall to get the light switch. A leathery hand choked my throat before I could even register the shadows had come alive.

My hands shot up and clawed his arm, but the man knocked me off balance and cinched me up close to his body from behind. The door shut behind me taking the last wedge of hallway light with it.

I was plunged into a heart-pounding darkness but now there were stars shooting around the corners of my eyes from the pressure on my jugular.

"Did you forget about the Sandman?" the stranger's voice said.

I tried to say *hey* or *what* or something but my throat just clucked.

"Don't forget the Sandman," he said. "Children shouldn't forget about the man who puts them to sleep."

My nails tried to dig into his rock-like forearm, except I really had chewed my nails down to nubs.

I got control of my mind and let my rigid muscles go slack.

This was the messenger I'd been watching for, let him give the message so this event could be done with.

The stars kept shooting out of the sides of my eyes.

The guy's breath ran across the top of my left ear and smelled like sunflower seeds and my lungs started screaming for air but I couldn't make a sound and my muscles lit back on fire and I started kicking and hitting but the guy was a concrete pillar.

He choked me out.

When I woke up I was on the floor beside my room's front door just like I'd walked in and collapsed on my own. I felt terribly nauseous and really frustrated. The neck is so vulnerable and I'm tired of it being used against me.

Then a wave of emotions washed over me and I started shaking.

I said, "Hello?" I guess I just wanted to know if anybody else was in the room or if the abuse was over for now.

It was over.

I got myself into the bathroom and locked the door. I got the shower water on before I started sobbing.

My emotions had just jumped on the roller coaster from happy to freaked out. I needed to call my husband Mac. I needed to hear his deep and loving voice and imagine his protective arms around me. But if I told him where I was he would drive like a bat out of hell to come get me and I knew I wouldn't talk him out of it.

And he'd bring his target pistol.

I'd told Mac a long time ago that I'd tried to kill my dad one night as a teenager. I pulled a trigger at his face with a handgun I thought was loaded. It had just clicked.

I punched the glass mirror.

I know it was a stupid thing to do, punching glass.

Long ago I used to be suicidal, and I'd think—if I don't kill myself, who will?

I've tried to leave all that self-destructive stuff behind me, but sometimes it still crops up.

I looked hard in the mirror through the blood spatter of my busted knuckle. I'd need a Band-Aid. I caught my own brown eyes and pinned them down like the enemy. That's when I truly realized what's different about me. My eyes are filled with light.

That's what's different about my palms and the same knobby knuckles and the middle finger that curves like a bow. I touch with love and healing.

I think I cried harder after that, but it was with relief. Sometimes the pain of the past makes me do stupid things. I got myself under control, made a hot cup of black coffee, and went back to work on my novel.

When I opened up my laptop a yellow post-it was stuck on the screen. It flittered to the floor. The warning said: *Be careful what you say*.

Well, obviously. I wasn't switching to non-fiction now, if that's what the bastards meant.

Sometimes the dark side just gets stuck on repeat.

I wrote for four days straight. Actually, that's not true. I lost the third day because I got drunk and then hung-over, got myself under control again—and then typed like a madwoman on fire the fourth day to make up for it.

———

I DROVE UP TO MY DAD'S HOUSE AND PARKED IN FRONT OF HIS house.

It was a gorgeous sunny day and when I popped out of the truck I didn't feel like the sniper rifle was sighted on my head anymore. The Order had given me their message, oh high-and-mighty elite, powerful people. It was more about what they *didn't* say.

They *didn't* say go home. They *didn't* say stop writing. They just said be careful and that meant I was in their territory but so far I was okay. I knew I was smart enough to know the edge of my playpen and not climb out.

I'd played this crime game all my life, and just as much as I'd been warned—I'd also been given permission.

When my dad answered the door I told him I'd finished my novel. I stepped into his house, and the smell was still there, but I didn't smell it as much.

He had his oil paint set out and asked if I'd like to have a white canvas. I dropped my *art, whatever* attitude and accepted a long, wide brush. It was a strange moment when I considered blood red and what I could have done with the goop of black paint from the tube. But that seemed a little inflammatory.

How about a peaceful landscape?

We painted and chatted and I thought *I'm standing here in this house with the tortured man who tortured me and I'm doing okay*. My dad has a happy-go-lucky sense of humor that I appreciate. I see where I got it from.

Sometimes you need to tally up the positive things.

I finished my novel and emailed it off to New York.

I spent the last four days hanging with my dad at his

house. I stopped reaching for my serrated key. I tried his delicious chili. I even used his restroom—though I did the hovering thing and didn't *actually* sit. Of course I used the lock, too.

I'd been searching for that thin line between fear and courage. That balance point. I think I found it.

It didn't cost me anything to relish the humor in my life. I was born of a man who chose darkness, and I became a woman of light.

Maybe I should thank him for the challenge. It made me who I am. I even left my landscape paining for him to hang in his art gallery. A bunch of sheep grazing inside a country fence, and one outside the pen.

That's me.

I even hugged him gently goodbye. I felt his body language, I watched the look in his eyes. He looked brighter, just a little. It might not be that long before he dies, and if he can forgive himself maybe he can make it to a lesser hell. Or even the light?

I think that would be good.

It's not like we became friends. It's not like I would see him again. But all things aside, he's a human being and so am I.

I packed up and headed back to Los Angeles and my life and my friends and my future. My monster experiment was a success. I don't have the answers. I've only got more questions.

But if we don't help them heal, who will?

ABOUT THE AUTHOR

When Valerie Brook was a little girl her parent's television blew out one night just as the news broadcast ended. For some mysterious and fateful reason, they never fixed it. Not for five years. And during those five years her mother read to her nearly every night; filling her mind with distant lands, magical creatures, and heroic courage. This seeded Val's childhood dream to be a writer.

When she's not writing fiction, she enjoys photography, riding motorcycles and dreaming about living in a world where people are sane.

FOR MORE BOOKS:

VALERIEBROOK.COM

ALSO BY VALERIE BROOK

FOR MORE BOOKS:

VALERIEBROOK.COM

Printed in the USA
CPSIA information can be obtained
at www.ICGtesting.com
JSHW032326271223
54272JS00003B/106

9 781942 026136